Nathaniel Hawthorne, Alexander H. Japp

Memoir of Nathaniel Hawthorne

with stories now first published in this country

Nathaniel Hawthorne, Alexander H. Japp

Memoir of Nathaniel Hawthorne
with stories now first published in this country

ISBN/EAN: 9783337228224

Printed in Europe, USA, Canada, Australia, Japan

Cover: Foto ©Raphael Reischuk / pixelio.de

More available books at **www.hansebooks.com**

Memoir of

Nathaniel Hawthorne

WITH STORIES

NOW FIRST PUBLISHED IN THIS COUNTRY

BY

H. A. PAGE

LONDON
HENRY S. KING & CO., 65 CORNHILL
1872

PREFACE.

THE circumstance that I have had access to several American Magazines, hardly of recent date, and to the various American editions of Nathaniel Hawthorne's works, has enabled me to trace out several short stories and sketches of his which, though acknowledged by him, have never been reprinted here or given to English readers. Believing that a certain literary and a very distinct auto-biographic value attaches itself to every page that Hawthorne wrote, I devoted my first leisure time to expanding and revising, in the light of this later and more extended search, a short memoir of him, which I had previously written. The results are, for the most part, contained in this volume.

As to the new matter, a few words may be allowed me here. 'Mother Rigby's Pipe,' if it is not one of the most striking and generally interesting of Hawthorne's tales, is decidedly characteristic. Here we have an illustration of his unique power of concentrating himself on one point and throwing down on it from all sides the most capricious lights of fancy; while yet never ceasing to moralise through a delicate medium of allegory. The meanings are profound enough, but the humour is of the finest and relieves their presence; gently lighting up the whole now and then, suddenly, as a smile will unexpectedly pass over a pensive countenance. It required no little skill so to use witchcraft as to gently satirise, by means of it, the artificialities and follies of the present. There are many meanings in the story, but the leading one it is not easy to miss. The chief secondary lesson is worth pointing out—that simplicity alone is the unfailing guarantee and accompaniment of true insight. The tale too abounds in separate thoughts, claiming to be well kept in the memory; as, witness Hawthorne's remark that 'feeble and torpid natures, being incapable of better inspiration, need to be stirred up by fear.'

The 'Passages from a Relinquished Work' only professedly takes this form to serve his purpose the better. Exquisite also in its delicate humour, it exhibits, through the thinnest of dramatic disguises, the effect on his fiction of what he called his puritanic blood and training—leading him to seek out, and give prominence to, obscure points—matters relating to the inner life, in fact—and to disregard the more obvious sources of interest.

The first of the 'Sketches from Memory' has direct critical value in its relation to the story of 'The Great Carbuncle,' as students of Hawthorne and thoughtful readers will at once discover for themselves. 'April Fools' shows how, even when the editor's pen was in his hand, and when the theme was common-place and hackneyed, he could not escape from moralising and unconscious allegory.

A warm word of acknowledgment for help received is due to Mr. Fields' 'Yesterdays with Authors;' though the bulk of this memoir is derived from other sources and was written before Mr. Fields' sketches first appeared. I have not, however, hesitated to draw in a fact or characteristic utterance from this source. So complete is Mr. Fields' sketch of Hawthorne, and so excellent is the spirit in which it is written, that this effort of mine would have been rendered unnecessary, if it had not been that the form with which Mr. Fields contents himself, limits him to separate points and anecdotes, with no real connection in time. If he had thrown his materials into a definitely-connected shape before publishing in book form, I fear my little endeavour would have been forestalled, and doubtless by a worthier product. But Mr. Fields' method

has led him into errors, which become confus-
ing when one is in earnest search for the real
facts of Hawthorne's life. One instance will
illustrate what is meant. Mr. Fields at p. 45,
writes thus :—' When Hawthorne was a little
more than fourteen the family moved to
Raymond in the state of Maine.' And then,
near to the end of his sketch, he says, in re-
porting Hawthorne's words : ' He said at an
early age he accompanied his mother and
sister to the township in Maine, which his
grandfather had purchased. That, he continued, was the happiest period of his life,
and it lasted till he was thirteen, when he was
sent to school in Salem.' Hawthorne could
not have been more than eleven when the
family removed to Raymond; for certainly he
went to school at Salem when he came
back from there.

Had space allowed, I might have been
tempted to illustrate in fuller detail the peculiar way in which Hawthorne continually

returned on his own ideas. But this itself would have needed almost a volume, for it would have been nothing else than an exhaustive analysis of his novels, in the light of biographical facts and of his note books. When, for example, he temporarily threw aside 'Septimius' in dissatisfaction, he could not, along with it, 'rid his bosom of the perilous stuff' of 'deathlessness.' He simply found relief in 'Pansie,' which we now know was to be a statement of the same idea from what he regarded, however, as the healthier side. As Septimius aimed at conquering the ' common fate' by *charms* and was miserably defeated; so old Dr. Dolliver was unconsciously to conquer death by the mightier spell of natural affection. There was an old saying that a man could not die so long as he kept his feet; so Hawthorne, by Dr. Dolliver, doubtless meant to illustrate, in his own striking way, that 'love alone confers immortality,' which, indeed, was with him a kind of favourite dogma.

I entertain hope that there are not a few who will sympathise with my honest effort to throw light on Hawthorne's life and character, and to render his writings yet more familiar to English readers.

H. A. P.

CONTENTS.

BIOGRAPHICAL SKETCH.

NATHANIEL HAWTHORNE was born in the quaint old town of Salem, on July 4, 1804. There is something striking in the circumstance that the man who was to give New England fresh life in literature—to garner up in words most rare and fine, 'the light and colour of every historic day that had dawned and set in it'—saw the light as the 4th of July bells were ringing, and on the very ground where took place the weirdest events with which early story in the Massachusetts colony is associated. For he was a direct descendant of the Puritan persecutors—of that Hawthorne who hunted down the Quakers, and of that Justice John Hawthorne, the son, who, strong in the idea of at once serving the state and propitiating heaven, was not loth to give sentence against the witches, and has been so faithfully pictured by Longfellow in his tragedy of 'The Salem Farms.'

B

Whether it were that these grim persecutions of Quakers and witches were doomed to bear no lucky fruit for those who had taken part in them, or even for their descendants, as time went on, it would be hard to say ; but, at any rate, the worldly success of the Hawthorne race did not long continue. The family declined rapidly, and ran on for generations in a long line of mariners and inconsiderable merchants ; all of them being blessed with but little prosperity, contrasted with the high position which their forefathers had held among the first settlers of Massachusetts. ' From father to son, for above a hundred years, they followed the sea: a gray-headed shipmaster in each generation, retiring from the quarter-deck to the homestead, while a boy of fourteen took the hereditary place before the mast, confronting the salt spray, and the gale which had blustered against his sire and grandsire. The boy also, in due time, passed from the forecastle to the cabin, spent a tempestuous manhood, and returned from his world-wanderings to grow old and die, and mingle his dust with the natal earth.'

Thus writes Hawthorne himself, so intent upon the past, that it was not required of him to specify there the very important circumstance that the last of the line of sailors never did come back to Salem to lay his dust by the side of his kindred in the natal earth. Captain Nathaniel Hawthorne, his father, who had had due share of the world-wanderings—a brave and fearless man—never returned from one of his long voyages. He died some say at Calcutta, some say at Surinam, after two girls and a boy had been born to him ; he having married a woman of sensibility, strong character, and remarkable beauty of person—Elizabeth Clarke Manning—who had also come of a good Salem family. The death of her husband cast such a gloom over her life, that she remained a sorrowful recluse ever afterwards ; the dark shade of her sorrow no doubt falling heavily on the boy, and preparing him to receive the more readily the weird impressions which Salem was so well fitted to produce.

We read that Hawthorne's mother had 'many characteristics in common with her distinguished son, she also being a very reserved and thoughtful person.' We shall see that there was a good deal both of father and mother in the boy's temperament ; for we are told that the elder Hawthorne, though an excellent sailor, and perfectly contented with his sphere, was yet a 'devourer of books,' and would take away with him on his long voyages volumes and pamphlets of a most unlikely character for one in such an occupation. With these he mainly passed his spare time on board ship; for he was ' inclined to melancholy and very reticent.'

The Mannings were next door neighbours of the Hawthornes in Union Street, but had secured some property elsewhere. So it came about that the young Nathaniel—left fatherless at four years of age—was much thrown upon his mother's people, spending his early years mostly under the care of his uncle, Robert Manning, and often living on an estate which belonged to them near to the town of Raymond, not far from Sebago Lake, in Maine. One can easily imagine the glee with which the boy would set out on his journeys, and how, boy-like, he would be just as eager to return to the old house in Union Street, near to the Long Wharf, the centre of the now dwindling foreign trade of Salem, which was flowing fast into the ports of New York and Boston; notwithstanding that Salem could boast honours in that regard of which they could not deprive it. The first American ship for India and China sailed from its port, and Salem ships opened the trade with Holland and the South Seas. It had still its Custom House and its wharves, and, though some of its once busy courts

were grass-grown, the seafaring flavour clung about
the whole town. The recurrent noise and stir of
traffic would please the lad vastly after the quiet
of Manning's Folly, as the country-house was
named, with its large rooms and rambling passages.

But Salem had other interest besides its trade,
not unlikely to exercise a powerful influence over
his quick, sensitive mind. It was redolent of the
past. The spirit of New England seemed to hover
over it. Some of its quaint wooden houses had
been the scene of tragic story ; for they had been
the abodes of Endicotts, Corwins, Curwins, Gedneys,
Gardners, Higginsons, Hutchisons, Mathers, and
Hathornes—names that carry a whiff of New
England air with them. The Witch-house, where,
in 1692, the old women who had the misfortune to
be ugly as well as old were tried and mercilessly
condemned for witchcraft, by the pious fathers of
New England, still stood ; and one could sit upon
the Gallows-hill, where the witches were hung, and
look out upon the far-stretching sea, as one mused
on the ways of Providence, and the strange changes
that time brings to the birth. The memory of
these witchcraft tortures and executions has thrown
a kind of ghostly spell over Salem, exactly of the

kind to entrance the imagination of a boy like Hawthorne.

And he soon became a voracious reader of the very sort of books calculated to deepen the impression that would inevitably be made by the stories he would constantly hear. An early accident, too, withdrew him from companions of the same age, and tended to breed the shyness and love of solitude by which he was ever afterwards characterised. When between eight and nine years of age, while playing at bat and ball, he was struck in the foot and lamed, so that he was compelled to use crutches. Up to this time he had been a lively boy, entering with enthusiasm into all kinds of games and fun. We are told that, during his lameness, he found all his delight in books, lying flat upon the carpet and reading whatever he could lay his hands on. It is not without significance, in one respect, that the 'Castle of Indolence' was a special favourite, and that the first book he bought with his own money was 'The Faërie Queen.' But still more significant is his fondness for Bunyan's 'Pilgrim.' Whenever he went to visit his grandmother Hawthorne he used to take the old family copy to a large chair in a corner of the room, near a window, and read by the hour without once speaking ; no one ever interfering with him, or asking him any questions. Thus early he used to invent long stories of a wild and fanciful character, and would speak of the travels he would undertake, and the adventures he would engage in, when he became a man, a suggestive forecast of that mixture of love for shy studious retirement, and hunger for practical contact with men, and with new scenes and situations, which characterised him to the end.

He had not long recovered from his lameness when he was seized by an illness which deprived him of the use of his limbs, so that once again he was only able to move about by the aid of crutches. But all this while his education was solicitously superintended by his uncle Robert. When the boy could no longer go to school, he engaged the best masters, who regularly came and heard him his lessons. The most notable of these was Joseph Worcester, the well-known author of the dictionary.

When he was between ten and eleven, his mother retired with him and his sisters to the property of her family, near Sebago Lake. She longed for more complete retirement than Salem would allow ; and she could scarcely have found a more suitable spot than Manning's Folly. It was almost shut in by the great pine-trees, which, when

the house had first been built, had been partially
cleared away, but had, in course of years, almost
regained their old dominion. The lasting effect of
his few years' residence here Hawthorne has himself put on record in most characteristic words: ' I
lived in Maine like a bird in the air,' he says, ' so
perfect was the freedom I enjoyed. But it was
there I first got my cursed habits of solitude.' We
can easily imagine the dreamy dark-eyed youth,
haunted by sad thoughts of his mother's singular
circumstances and all unjoyous life. Unable to
frame into words the sympathy he could not but
feel, he endeavoured to find relief in outdoor
exercise and observation of nature. ' During the
moonlight nights he would skate until midnight
all alone upon the Sebago Lake, with the deep
shadow of the icy hills on either hand. When he
found himself far away from his home and weary
with skating, he would take refuge in a log-cabin,
where half a tree would be burning on the log-
hearth. He would sit in the ample chimney and
look at the stars through the great aperture which
the flame went roaring up. " Ah," he said, " how
well I recall the summer days also when with my
gun I roamed at will through the woods of Maine.
How sad middle life looks, to people of erratic

temperaments. Everything is beautiful in youth, for all things are allowed to it." ' These days spent in the piny solitudes of Maine without companions —skating in the moonlight, and shooting in the long summer afternoons, have left witness of themselves in many a shadowy picture and sombre glimpse of natural grandeur.

At fourteen, he returned to Salem to attend school, where, under the care of his uncle, he was prepared for college. Here he took great delight in wandering at night about the old town, or on the sea-beach, his imagination full of the weird memories that clustered about its weather-stained, wooden-gabled houses. He was quick to learn, and showed that he was made of the very material for a scholar : but he had little ambition to surpass others, and was not likely to strain a faculty in the keen race of competition. Even at this time he was marked by quiet solicitude for the satisfaction of real self-development rather than by any concern for the applause of others.

While yet only sixteen, Hawthorne was sent by his uncle to Bowdoin College, in Maine, where he studied with great success. Half a lifetime afterwards, his teachers remembered the excellence of his English and Latin compositions. He had for fellow-students Longfellow, Cheever, Franklin Pierce, and Horatio Bridge. All these acknowledged to have received from him a singularly powerful influence. Bridge entered the navy, and his 'Journal of an African Cruiser' was edited by Hawthorne, who again dedicated to Bridge his volume entitled 'The Snow Image.' In the course of the dedicatory letter, he gives this exquisite glimpse of himself as a student :—

'On you, if on no other person, I am entitled to rely, to sustain the position of my dedicatee. If anybody is responsible for my being at this day an author, it is yourself. I know not whence your faith came ; but, while we were lads together at a country college, gathering blue-berries, in study-hours, under those tall academic pines ; or watching the great logs, as they tumbled along the current of the Androscoggin ; or shooting pigeons and gray squirrels in the woods; or bat-fowling in the summer twilight; or catching trouts in that shadowy little stream which I suppose is still wandering riverward through the forest,—though you and I will never cast a line in it again,—two idle lads in short (as we need not fear to acknowledge now), doing a hundred things that the Faculty never heard of, or else it had been the worse for us ; still it was your prognostic of your friend's destiny that he was to be a writer of fiction.'

Hawthorne made close friends of several of his fellow-students. In their society it would seem that his confirmed shyness and reserve, to a great extent, vanished. He was then famous for his manly beauty and for his feats of physical strength. His frame would have given the impression of a soldier or a sportsman rather than of a student, had it not been for 'a certain reserve and grace which rendered the size and strength of frame unobtrusive.'

Here we meet with another illustration of the truth, that those who are destined to impress remarkable characters most deeply, often themselves remain obscure or become distinguished in ways that tend to make one's surprise at their early power all the greater. Franklin Pierce, it is evident, had then more influence with Hawthorne than all the rest. Pierce himself, as everyone knows, became a lawyer, later turned a soldier, and then a politician; for in the States every profession seems to point to politics as a final goal. It is clear that, with the best desire to look favourably on his strange, though successful career, it was not quite so invariably spotless and high-minded as his early friend Hawthorne was inclined to paint it. Hawthorne could see no fault in Frank, his old class-mate. When there was a feeling in the States that Pierce had compromised himself, Hawthorne set about writing a defence of him, and the defence took the shape of a biography—certainly one of the most characteristic of biographies. It is a slight volume, but it stands entirely by itself for its transparent candour, its ease and frankness ; and yet it is not wanting in a certain worldly shrewdness and a sort of unconscious casuistry. It is of value to us because of the references to their early life which it contains. Indeed, the one substantial plea Hawthorne gives for writing it, is that he did intimately know Pierce when both were boys. He thus apologises, in the third person, for the bold course he has taken of justifying his friend :—

'This species of writing [political biography] is too remote from the author's customary occupations —and, he may add, from his tastes—to be very satisfactorily done, without more time and practice than he would be willing to spend for such a purpose. If this little biography have any value, it is probably of another kind—as the narrative of one who knew the individual of whom he treats, at a period of life when character could be read with undoubting accuracy, and who, consequently, in judging of the motives of his subsequent conduct, has an advantage over much more competent observers, whose knowledge of the man may have commenced at a later date.'

Here, as elsewhere, of course, we cannot detach Hawthorne from the subject of which he writes. In every touch he reveals himself: if we only look closely and sympathetically, we read as much of Hawthorne's life at college as we do of Pierce's. If Pierce has frank and friendly traits, they can only be brought out by a glance at the shyness which they overcame ; if he was fond of sport and pleasure, it can only be acknowledged in connection with the infectious and inspiriting influence which he constantly carried with him. How fresh and beautiful and friendly, and yet how ingenuously self-confessing, is this touch :—

' He [Pierce] was then a youth, with the boy and man in him, vivacious, mirthful, slender, of a fair complexion, with light hair that had a curl in it ; his bright and cheerful aspect made a kind of sunshine both as regarded its radiance and warmth, *insomuch that no shyness of disposition in his associates could well resist its influence.'*

If Hawthorne's shyness was conquered so completely by Pierce, then Pierce must have possessed remarkable force of character, and winning charms of disposition. It is clear, too, that he did possess such. He led Hawthorne, the recluse, to share his sports with him; under his enthusiasm Hawthorne actually became a volunteer, arrayed himself in uniform, and went to exercise! It seems so utterly foreign to our ideas of Hawthorne, to see him as a young man strutting about in *dilettante* soldiership. He himself seems to look back to those days and their pastimes with a sad, flickering smile, not, however, without token of pleasure and satisfaction in the remembrance. With all his graceful, earnest playfulness, he writes:—

'I remember, likewise, that the only military service of my life was as a private soldier in a college company of which Pierce was one of the officers. He entered into this latter business, or pastime, with an earnestness with which I could not pretend to compete, and at which, perhaps, he would now be inclined to smile.'

So passed the pleasant days at Bowdoin; faithful records of which were to remain in many ways. Hawthorne left it with a new and deeper sense of friendship than he had almost believed himself capable of. It was something that he could carry into his after self-sought solitude such kindly thoughts as he did carry thence. They had their own share, doubtless, in saving him from the cynicism which often seemed to threaten him. After he had graduated with honour he retired from this 'country college' to Salem, in 1825, as 'though it were for him the inevitable centre of the universe ;' and here, in his native place, he lived the life of a recluse—'passing the day alone in his room, writing wild tales, most of which he destroyed, and walking out at night.'

Soon after he left college he wrote some stories which he called 'Seven Tales of my Native Land.' The motto which he chose for the title-page was, 'We are Seven,' from Wordsworth. 'My informant read the tales in manuscript,' writes Mr. Fields, 'and says some of them were very striking, particularly one or two Witch Stories,' which may readily be believed. As soon as the little book was well prepared for the press, he deliberately threw it into the fire, and sat by to see its destruction.

But, in spite of this severity with the products of his own pen—a thing unusual enough with young writers—he still went on busily producing ; and, before very long, he published anonymously a slight romance with the motto from Southey, 'Wilt thou go with me ?' He never acknowledged the book, but it shows plainly the natural bent of his mind. 'It is a dim, dreamy tale, such as a Byron-struck youth of the time might have written, except for that startling self-possession of style, and cold analysis of passion, rather than sympathy with it, which showed no imitation, but remarkable original power.' The same lurid gloom overhangs it that shadows all his works. It is uncanny ; the figures of the romance are not persons, they are passions, emotions, spiritual speculations. He met all requests to republish it in later days with a firm refusal, even begging his friend, Mr. Fields, never to mention the dead book to him again.

A desire for adventure, for practical contact with men, is in him singularly combined with shyness and reticence. It is significant and worthy of remark that about this time he applied for a situation under Commodore Wilkes to go on an exploring expedition. He did not succeed in obtaining an appointment, and regarded this as a great misfortune ; for he had been volubly enthusiastic about the wonderful things he should do, if he were permitted to join the voyagers. He had to remain yet a while longer in Salem.

It was now that the old town put forth her full power of fascination on him. It is told how that

he would decline invitations to the drawing-rooms
of the better class, and would seek out illiterate
old friends, and would familiarly hob-nob with
them. The gloomy mystery of Puritan life and
character had fallen on a sensitive imagination in
many ways prepared to take its impress. Struggling by day to unravel the obscurer mysteries of
the spiritual life, he would find fresh suggestions of
weird horror in the sombre monuments that met
his gaze as he wandered, ghost-like, through Salem
streets at dead of night. It was during this period,
when so much was at work to colour and give
permanent bent to his genius, that the ' Twice Told
Tales ' were mostly written. They clearly tell of
the influences which were most powerful. They
either concern themselves with the analysis of mixed
and morbid conditions of feeling, or they quaintly
describe scenes of the olden time, with a gleam of
sunshine thrown into the picture, that, like a little
stream half hidden under leaves in a shadowy pine
wood, glimmers here and there only to deepen the
sense of sombre loneliness, when the glimpse of it
is momentarily lost again.

' I sat down by the wayside of life, like a man
under enchantment, and a shrubbery sprang up
around me, and the bushes grew to be saplings, and

the saplings became trees, until no exit appeared possible, through the entangling depths of my obscurity. And there perhaps I should be sitting at this moment, with the moss on the imprisoning tree-trunks, and the yellow leaves of more than a score of autumns piled above me, if it had not been for you.'—Referring to his early friend, Horatio Bridge.

Bridge and O'Sullivan, who was then editor of 'The Democratic Review,' urged him to contribute to its pages, and thus an efficient way was first opened to him for contact with the public. But the great public did not at once get into raptures over the airy and allegoric pabulum with which Hawthorne was most inclined to supply it. He himself was pleased with the warm recognition of a limited circle, and wrote of himself, afterwards, with a touch of semi-cynical pride, as having been for long years, 'the most obscure man of letters in America.'

In 1836, he went to Boston to edit the 'American Magazine of Useful Knowledge,' for which he was to be paid a salary of six hundred dollars a year. 'The proprietors soon became insolvent, so that he received nothing, but he kept on just the same as if he had been paid regularly. The plan of the work proposed by the publishers of the magazine admitted no fiction into its pages. The magazine, [consisting of forty pages a month], was printed on coarse paper, and was illustrated by engravings painful to look at. There were no contributors except the editor, and he wrote [nearly] the whole of every number.' Short biographical sketches of eminent men, descriptive papers, scraps of scientific information, historical narratives, and now and then a bit of music, filled up its pages ; and the presence of Hawthorne is not otherwise to be detected than in an occasional felicity of style—an aptly turned sentence or a happy characterisation. No doubt his fine taste was often offended by the style of illustration dealt in, but he went on from March till August, sometimes throwing in, notwithstanding all these disadvantages, a very characteristic little paper. The magazine looks terribly dull in spite of the publisher's claim that it was 'illustrated in the best style.' However, Hawthorne's patience at last gave way, and he resigned. In the note in which he took leave of his readers, he relieved himself from certain responsibilities in these terms :—'In some few cases perhaps the interests of the work might have been promoted by allowing the editor the privilege of a veto, at least, on all engravings which were to be presented to the public under his auspices, and for which his taste and judgment would inevitably be held responsible. In general, however, the embellishments have done no discredit either to the artists or their employers.'

Through this magazine, Hawthorne became known to many members of the more influential class, and doubtless his connection with it helped towards his appointment as collector at the Custom-house of Boston. But still he was to the great reading public a comparatively unknown man.

Even when the ' Twice Told Tales ' were gathered together and published in book form—the first volume having appeared in 1839—they produced little or no impression, notwithstanding that the critics were ready to proclaim the advent of a new literary force. Longfellow, ever alert to what is excellent and eager to see an old fellow-student duly appreciated, was among the reviewers, having written a very discriminating but highly laudatory notice of the work in the ' North American Review.'

After Hawthorne had had eighteen months' trial of life as an assistant collector in the Custom-house at Boston, the duties of which he seems to have discharged with singular patience and discreetness,

he wrote thus whilst he was a temporary inmate of
the Union Street family mansion :—

'Now I begin to understand why I was im-
prisoned so many years in this lonely chamber, and
why I could never break through the viewless bolts
and bars; for if I had sooner made my escape
into the world, I should have grown hard and
rough, and been covered with earthly dust, and my
heart might have become callous by rude en-
counters with the multitude. . . . But living in
solitude till the fulness of time was come, I still kept
the dew of my youth and the freshness of my heart.
. . . I used to think I could imagine all passions,
all feelings and states of the heart and mind; but
how little did I know! *Indeed, we are but shadows;
we are not endowed with real life, and all that
seems most real about us is but the thinnest substance
of a dream, till the heart be touched. That touch
creates us—then we begin to be—thereby we are
beings of reality, and inheritors of eternity.*

'When we shall be endowed with our spiritual
bodies, I think that they will be so constituted that
we may send thoughts and feelings any distance in
no time at all, and transfuse them warm and fresh
into the consciousness of those whom we love. But,
after all, perhaps it is not wise to intermix fantastic

ideas with the reality of affection. Let us content ourselves to be earthly creatures, and hold communion of spirit in such modes as are ordained to us.'

In 1841 Hawthorne lost his place through political changes, and it was then that he ventured on the bold experiment of residence at Brook Farm, which had a far more intimate bearing on his mental development than almost any other of the outward changes of his life. It is scarcely possible that a man of his temperament could have embarked in a socialistic experiment expecting very much from it, in any other form than as presenting a medium for fresh observation of character. There is a tone of hopefulness in the first entries of his journal, and yet a sort of cynicism seems to surcharge them almost unconsciously.

'Through faith,' he says, 'I persist in believing that spring and summer will come in their due season ; but the *unregenerated man shivers within me and suggests a doubt whether I may not have wandered within the precincts of the Arctic Circle, and chosen my heritage among everlasting snows.* . . . Provide yourself with a good stock of furs, and if you can obtain the skin of a Polar bear, you will find it a very suitable summer dress for this region.'

It has been said that Brook Farm was an attempt to practically exhibit the 'transcendental' ideas which had been eloquently proclaimed, and that Emerson, the apostle of the new ideas, though interested in Brook Farm and a constant visitor, did not regard himself as being called to organise expedients for the practical embodiments of these ideas. But this would scarcely account for Hawthorne's having taken part in the enterprise. He was singularly free from being subject to 'transcendental' enthusiasm, and, while a warm friend of Emerson, did not suffer himself to be moved an iota from his own groove of poised and self-centred, yet half-morbid meditation. Clearly Hawthorne's presence at Brook Farm had not been dictated by any great hope of a regeneration of humanity, such as inspired Dana, and Ripley, and Pratt, who were professed enthusiasts in the scheme—men who had devoured the works of Owen and Fourier, and fancied that their ideas only needed the infusion of sound religious sentiment, to secure such a permanence as had been denied to former schemes of the kind. Hawthorne was too sharp an observer of human nature to cherish such dreams as these. Besides, he was by nature sceptical of anything which interfered with the free development of

natural tendencies. He had no faith in philanthropy. He was a conservative and an aristocrat
simply in virtue of that wistful scepticism which
made him ever doubtful of new courses. But at
the same time there was in Hawthorne a very
decided vein of curiosity and a strong need for
contact with fresh scenes and situations. He fell
on torpid moods, on periods of 'suspended animation,' as he himself has called them, and needed to
be quickened out of them by contact with prosaic
and extraordinary conditions of life. We believe
that Hawthorne expected to find such in Brook
Farm. Not that he consciously framed to himself
the reasons for his going thither. He went in
obedience to a dictate of his nature—the same as
had reconciled him so completely to coal-weighing
at Boston, and was yet to reconcile him to the surveyor's work at Salem and the consul's work at
Liverpool. It was that element in his character
which led to the following confession, which reap-
pears in manifold forms throughout the more
personal portions of his stories and his journals :—

' It contributes greatly towards a man's moral
and intellectual health, to be brought into habits of
companionship with individuals unlike himself, who
care little for his pursuits, and whose sphere and

abilities he must go out of himself to appreciate. The accidents of my life have often offered me this advantage.'

Yet so far, we are compelled to believe there was a disinterested motive behind Hawthorne's movements while at Brook Farm. He took his fair share of the work ; and the first savings of his pen were put into the scheme. But he could not devote himself to it, as he had hoped. He was involuntarily an observer rather than a co-worker. Mr. Noyes, in his ' History of American Socialisms,' waxes rather wroth against Hawthorne ; but he fails to appreciate the man's nature in this regard, and, consequently, tends to do him an injustice. ' This brilliant Community,' says Mr. Noyes, ' has a right to complain that its story should have to be told by aliens. Emerson, who was not a member of it, nor in sympathy with the socialistic movement to which it abandoned itself, has volunteered a lecture of reminiscences ; and Hawthorne, who joined it only to jilt it, has given the world a poetico-sneering romance about it ; and that is all the first-hand information we have except what can be gleaned from obsolete periodicals. George William Curtis, though he was a member, coolly exclaims in " Harper's Magazine : "—" strangely enough, Hawthorne is likely to be the chief future authority upon the *romantic episode* of Brook Farm. Those who had it at heart more than he, whose faith and energy were all devoted to its development, and many of whom have every ability to make a permanent record, have never done so, and it is already so much a thing of the past, that it will probably never be done." In the name of history we ask, Why has not George William Curtis himself made the permanent record? Why has not George Ripley taken the story out of the mouths of the sneerers? Brook Farm might tell its story through him, for he *was* Brook Farm. It was George Ripley who took into his heart the inspiration of Dr. Channing, and went to work like a hero to make a fact of it; while Emerson stood by smiling incredulity. It was Ripley who put on his frock and carted manure, and set Hawthorne shovelling, and did his best for years to keep work going, that the Community might pay as well as play. It was no "picnic," or "romantic episode," or "chance meeting in a ship's cabin" to him. His whole soul was bent on making a *home* of it. If a man's first-born, in whom his heart is bound up, die at six years old, that does not turn the whole affair into a joke. There were others of the same spirit, but Ripley was the centre of them. Brook Farm came very near to being a *religious* Community. It inherited the spirit of Dr. Channing and of Transcendentalism. The inspiration in the midst of which it was born, was intensely literary, but also religious. The Brook Farmers refer to it as the " revival," the " *newness*," the " *renaissance*." There was evidently an afflatus on the men, and they wrote and acted as they were moved. " The Dial " was the original organ of this afflatus, and contains many articles that are edifying to Christians of good digestion.'

Hawthorne, no doubt, went to Brook Farm with hopes of results upon his own mind and character which were not realised ; and, therefore, all that was left for him was to leave it, as soon as he could in honour do so.

Looked at impartially, the ' Blithedale Romance' is a ' poetico-sneering one,' as Noyes has called it. It is a semi-cynical argument against all such schemes for reforming society. The moment Hawthorne went to Brook Farm, it seemed to become his main business to observe. He could not help himself; it consisted with his genius so to do. The redeeming point is that he deals as fairly by Miles Coverdale, his acknowledged *alter ego*, as by the rest.

Coverdale is put before us with his cold inquisitiveness, his incredulity, his determination to worm out the inmost secrets of all associated with him. Perhaps there is not a more characteristic touch in the work than we have in this passage, saturated as it is by a quiet cynical humour. He is speaking of the secret which seemed to lie sealed in Zenobia's heart, imparting a sort of falseness to her whole character and conduct.

'It irritated me, this self-complacent, condescending qualified approval and criticism of a system to which many individuals—perhaps as highly endowed as our gorgeous Zenobia—had contributed their all of earthly endeavour and loftiest aspirations. I determined to make proof if there were any spell that would exorcise her out of the part which she seemed to be acting. She should be compelled to give me a glimpse of something true—some nature, some passion, no matter whether right or wrong, provided it were real.'

And this was but a special instance of the exercise of a faculty which he speaks of generally as—
'That quality of the intellect and the heart which impelled me (*often against my own will, and to the detriment of my own comfort*) to live in other lives, and to endeavour—by generous sympathies, by

delicate intuitions, by taking note of things too slight for record, and by bringing my human spirit into manifold accordance with the companions God had assigned me—to learn the secret which was hidden even from themselves.'

In this way it was that Brook Farm served Hawthorne—in quite a different way, of course, from what he himself had expected. It gave him new views and impulses to literary production : it furnished him with several types of character :— ' The self-conceited philanthropist ; the high-spirited woman bruising herself against the narrow limitations of her sex ; the weakly maiden, whose trembling nerves endowed her with sibylline attributes ; the minor poet beginning life with strenuous aspirations which die out with his youthful fervour.'

' Really I should judge it to be twenty years since I left Brook Farm,' writes Hawthorne during a short holiday at Salem, in September 1841, ' and I take this to be one proof that my life there was an unnatural and unsuitable, and, therefore, an unreal one. It already looks like a dream behind me. The real Me was never an associate of the community ; there has been a spectral Appearance there, sounding the horn at day-break, and milking the cows, and hoeing potatoes, and raking hay, toiling in the sun, and doing me the honour to assume my name.   But the spectre was not myself. Nevertheless, it is somewhat remarkable that my hands have, during the past summer, grown very brown and rough, insomuch that many people persist in believing that I, after all, was the aforesaid spectral horn-sounder, cow-milker, potatoe-hoer, and hay-raker.   *But such people do not know a reality from a shadow.'*

Yet, in spite of all this, he returns to it, with full intent to profit, and to work to others' profit; only underneath all we see the same ever-recurrent vein of cynicism, and cold, self-removed observation :—

' Nothing here is settled ; everything is but beginning to arrange itself ; and though I would seem to have little to do with aught beside my own thoughts, still I cannot but partake of the ferment around me.   My mind will not be abstracted.   *I must observe, and think, and feel, and content myself with catching glimpses of things which may be wrought out hereafter.*   Perhaps it will be quite as well that I find myself unable to set seriously about literary occupation for the present.   It will be good to have a longer interval between my labour of the body, and that of the mind.   Meantime, I shall see *these people and their enterprise* under a new point of view, and, perhaps, be able to determine whether we have any call to cast in our lot with them.'

Hawthorne's connection with the first phase of the Brook Farm enterprise gives to it an importance which it would hardly otherwise have. The following sentences from an article in 'The Dial' by Miss Elizabeth Peabody, sketching the plan of the Community as an economy, may be read with interest : ' All who have property to take stock and receive a fixed interest thereon ; then to keep house or board in commons, as they shall severally desire, at the cost of provisions purchased at wholesale, or raised on the farm ; and all to labour in community, and be paid at a certain rate an hour [the labour was afterwards paid according to the work done], choosing their own number of hours, and their own kind of work. With the results of this labour and their interest, they are to pay their board, and also purchase whatever else they require at cost, at the warehouses of the Community. All labour, whether bodily or mental, is to be paid at the same rate of wages ; and none will be engaged in merely bodily labour. The hours of labour will be limited by a general law, and can be curtailed at the will of the individual still more ; and means will be given to all for intellectual improvement and for social intercourse, calculated to refine and expand.   The hours redeemed from labour by the Community will not be re-applied to the acquisition of wealth, but in the wealth itself which money should represent.   As a Community, it will traffic with the world at large, in the products of agricultural labour ; and it will sell education to as many young persons as can be domesticated in the families, and enter into the common life with their own children.   If the parents are unable to pay for them, the children will be educated gratuitously on condition of their agreeing to remain and work for the Community afterwards.'   The farm was about eight miles from Boston, and consisted of about 200 acres of land (unfortunately far from being of a productive character), and yet at the end of two years the Community possessed about 30,000 dollars; 22,000 of this being invested in the stock of the company, and in good loans at 6 per cent. interest.

But, gradually, and whilst Hawthorne was resident there, changes were introduced ; and the more experience of community life that he gained, the less he felt himself fitted to attach himself to it permanently.   Just when, as Noyes says, it was about to transform itself into a Fourieristic institution, Hawthorne, no doubt wisely, took his leave of it. With this retirement we may date the beginning of a new era in his life. He is hereafter less inclined to trust to ideas, and far less interested in them ; he seems determined to cultivate more than he has done acquaintance with the world as it goes. In 1843 he marries Miss Sophia Peabody, and retires to the Old Manse at Concord, which he has described so excellently at the opening of the 'Mosses from an Old Manse.'

He himself records that his life at this period was more like that of a boy externally than it had been since he was really a boy. 'It is usually supposed,' he proceeds, 'that the cares of life come with matrimony, but I seem to have cut off all care, and live on with as much easy trust in Providence as Adam could possibly have felt before he had learned that there was a world beyond Paradise. My chief anxiety consists in watching the prosperity of my vegetables, in observing how they are affected by the rain or sunshine, in lamenting the blight of one squash and rejoicing at the luxurious growth of another. It is as if the original relation between man and nature were restored in my case, and as if I were to look exclusively to her for the support of my Eve and myself, to trust to her for food and clothing, and all things needful with the full assurance that she will not fail me. . . Then [after breakfast] I pass down through an orchard to the river-side, and ramble along its margin in search of flowers. . . . Having made up my bunch I return home with them. Then I ascend to my study, and generally read, or perchance scribble, till the dinner-hour. In pleasant days the chief event of the afternoon is our walk. . . So comes the night, and I look back upon a day spent in what the world would call idleness, and for which I can myself suggest no more appropriate epithet, but which, nevertheless, I cannot feel to have been spent amiss. True, it might be a sin and shame, in such a world as ours, to spend a lifetime in this manner; but for a few summer weeks it is good to live as if this world were heaven. And so it is, and so it shall be, although in a little while, a flitting shadow of earthly care and toil will mingle itself with our realities.'

And so it speedily did. The responsibilities and necessities of a wedded home soon made themselves felt, and he cheerfully bent himself to his work. His residence at the Old Manse was a very productive period, though perhaps on the list it may not show so well as some others. 'Joys impregnate, sorrows bring forth,' says William Blake. Hawthorne here went through good journeyman-ship service, and laid in store of material to be wrought out in later days. A little of what he did at this time is classic. He wrote books of a less artistic character than he was well fitted to write, simply because the public would buy them; but here he wrote a portion of those 'True Stories told from Grandfather's Chair,' in which early American history is touched with so free yet so reverent a hand. The 'Mosses' were also gathered together here, and the charming introduction written whilst he was daily enjoying the exquisite scenery near Concord, and in close association with congenial minds like those of Emerson, Thoreau, and Long-fellow.

'During Hawthorne's first year's residence in Concord,' writes his friend, G. W. Curtis, who had left Brook Farm later to live at Concord, 'I had driven up with some friends to an æsthetic tea at Mr. Emerson's. It was in the winter, and a great wood fire blazed upon the hospitable hearth. There were various men and women of note assembled; and I, who listened attentively to all the fine things that were said, was for some time scarcely aware of a man, who sat upon the edge of the circle, a little withdrawn, his head slightly thrown forward upon his breast, and his black eyes clearly burning under his black brow. As I drifted down the stream of talk, this person, who sat silent as a shadow, looked to me as Webster might have looked had he been a poet—a kind of poetic Webster. He rose and walked to the window, and stood there quietly for a long time watching the dead-white landscape. No appeal was made to him; nobody looked after him; the conversation flowed steadily on, as if everyone understood that his silence was to be respected. It was the same thing at table. In vain the silent man imbibed æsthetic tea. Whatever fancies it inspired did not flower at his lips. But there was a light in his eye which assured me nothing was lost. So supreme was his silence, that it presently engrossed me to the exclusion of everything else. There was very brilliant discourse; but this silence was much more poetic and fascinating. Fine things were said by the philosophers; but much finer things were implied by the dumbness of this gentleman with heavy brows and black hair. When he presently rose and went, Emerson, with the slow, wise smile that breaks over his face

like day over the sky, said, " Hawthorne rides
well his horse of the night." '

Such was his life at this time, quiet, busy, productive. Sometimes, when Mrs. Hawthorne was
absent seeing her friends at Boston, he would dis-
miss the 'help,' and do all menial service for himself, such as cooking food, washing dishes, and
chopping wood. For this latter bit of work, indeed, he seems to have had quite a fancy. The
washing of dishes irritated him ; 'if the dishes
once cleaned would remain so for ever, one might
be content,' he says ; thus covering some of his own
awkwardness by the play of a humorous irony,
which is deeply characteristic of him. To the end,
much of the most pretentious effort of men seemed
to have its symbol in his washing of the dishes !

Near to the Old Manse had been fought a battle
in the War of Independence. The monument
erected in commemoration of it could be seen from
Hawthorne's garden ; but very significant are his
confessions with respect to these things, and the
manner in which other traces and traditions of the
war affected him.

'The monument, not more than twenty feet in
height, is such as it befitted the inhabitants of a
village to erect in illustration of a matter of local

interest rather than what was suitable to commemorate an epoch of national history. Still, by the fathers of the village this famous deed was done ; and their descendants might rightfully claim the privilege of building a memorial.

'A humbler token of the fight, yet a more interesting one than the granite obelisk, may be seen close under the stone wall which separates the battle ground from the precincts of the parsonage. It is the grave—marked by a small, moss-grown fragment of stone at the head and another at the foot—the grave of two British soldiers who were slain in the skirmish, and have ever since slept peacefully where Zechariah Brown and Thomas Davis buried them. Soon was their warfare ended ; a weary night-march from Boston, a rattling volley of musketry across the river, and then these many years of rest. In the long procession of slain invaders who passed into eternity from the battle-fields of the revolution, these two nameless soldiers led the way.

' Lowell, the poet, as we were once standing over this grave, told me a tradition in reference to one of the inhabitants below. The story has something deeply impressive, though its circumstances cannot altogether be reconciled with probability. A youth in the service of the clergyman happened to be chopping wood, that April morning, at the back of the Manse ; and when the noise of battle rang from side to side of the bridge he hastened across the intervening field to see what might be going forward. It is rather strange, by the way, that this lad should have been so diligently at work when the whole population of town and country were startled out of their customary business by the advance of the British troops. Be that as it might, the tradition says that the lad now left his task and hurried to the battle-field with the axe still in his hand. The British had by this time retreated ; the Americans were in pursuit ; and the late scene of strife was thus deserted by both parties. Two soldiers lay on the ground—one was a corpse ; but as the young New Englander drew nigh, the other Briton raised himself painfully upon his hands and knees, and gave a ghastly stare into his face. The boy—*it must have been a nervous impulse, without purpose, without thought, and betokening a sensitive, impressible nature rather than a hardened one*—the boy uplifted his axe and dealt the wounded soldier a fierce and fatal blow upon the head.

'I could wish that the grave might be opened ; for *I would fain know whether either of the skeleton soldiers has the mark of an axe in his skull. The story comes home to me like truth. Oftentimes, as an intellectual and moral exercise, I have sought to follow that poor youth through his subsequent career, and observe how his soul was tortured by the blood stain,* contracted as it had been before the long custom of war had robbed human life of its sanctity, and while it still seemed murderous to slay a brother-man. *This one circumstance has borne more fruit for me than all that history tells us of the fight.'*

It was not likely that such a thing should fail to make a deep impression on Hawthorne's mind, or that it should be lost in a literary point of view ; nor has it.

After nearly a three years' residence at the Old Manse, he was appointed by Mr. Bancroft to the office of Surveyor of the Port of Salem. All the world is familiar with the literary outcome of that period. 'The Scarlet Letter' is its never-dying memorial. He entered on his duties there in 1848, and in 1849 the first sketch of that unique production was shown to Mr. Fields, the famous publisher of Boston. But it illustrates well the character of Hawthorne, that he himself had no desire to seek the public favour again. The indifferent reception which 'The Twice Told Tales' had met with, and the slow sale even of his later efforts, seemed to have made him distrustful of his power to secure popularity, though it never seems to have made him doubtful of his destination as a burrower in the field of psychological romance. Mr. Fields, at once with the tact of a true literary adviser and the delicate consideration of a friend, managed to make the shy, reticent man confess to the existence of a hidden treasure, and did not leave till he had carried it away with him for perusal. The work was at once developed more fully under Mr. Field's advice, and no sooner was it published than it won its author fame.

Mr. Fields tells us that Hawthorne had intended to issue 'The Scarlet Letter' as the longest of a series of tales to be entitled ' Old Time Legends ; together with Sketches Experimental and Ideal.' When an extension of ' The Scarlet Letter' and a separate publication of it was proposed to him, he wrote :— ' If the book is made up entirely of " The Scarlet Letter," (I fear) it will be too sombre. I found it impossible to relieve the shadow of the story with so much light as I would gladly have thrown in. Keeping so close to its point as the tale does, and diversified no otherwise than by turning different sides of the same dark idea to the reader's eye, it will weary very many people and disgust some.   Is it safe, then, to stake the fate of the book entirely on this one chance ? A hunter loads his gun with a bullet and several buck shot ; and, following his sagacious example, it was my purpose to conjoin the one long story with half a dozen shorter ones, so that, failing to kill the public outright with my biggest and heaviest lump of lead, I might have other chances with the smaller bits individually and in the aggregate.   However, I am willing to leave these considerations to your judgment, and should not be sorry to have you decide for the separate publication.'

Of course the separate publication was decided for, and wisely; the 'Old Time Legends' taking their place among the 'Twice Told Tales ;' but the exquisite self-criticism here summed up in the words 'diversified no otherwise than by turning different sides of the same dark idea to the reader's eye '—is very noticeable and incisive, and shows at the same time a shrewd judgment of the popular taste.

At the end of three years' service at Salem Custom-house Hawthorne lost his place and retired to Lenox, where he lived a quiet, homely life. His family were now grown to boyhood and girlhood and were companionable. But he was much more inclined than before to be sociable ; and was often to be found among his neighbours at Mr. Dudley Field's, at Holmes's, or at Herman Melville's. Parties and excursions were frequently planned, and Hawthorne would sometimes on these occasions brighten and break out into flashes of quaint humour and anecdote. He was busy too. Here he wrote the 'Wonder Book,' and 'The House of the Seven Gables,' and thought a good deal about the 'Blithedale Romance' as he wandered among the Berkshire hills. He had always been much dependent on times and seasons ; and he confesses that he was now more so than ever. ' I shan't have the new story' ["The House of the Seven Gables "] 'ready by November,' he writes on October 1, 1850 ; 'for I am never good for anything in the literary way till after the first autumnal frost, which has somewhat such an effect on my imagination that it does on the foliage here about me,—multiplying and brightening its hues ; though they are likely to be sober and shabby enough, after all.'

Again he confesses :—

' I find the book' ['The House of the Seven Gables'] 'requires more care and thought than "The Scarlet Letter ;" also I have to wait oftener for a

mood. "The Scarlet Letter," being all in one tone,
I had only to get my pitch, and could then go on
interminably. Many passages of this work ought
to be finished with the minuteness of a Dutch
picture, in order to give them their proper effect.
Sometimes, when tired of it, it strikes me that the
whole is an absurdity, from beginning to end ; but
the fact is, in writing a romance, a man is always,
or always ought to be, careering on the utmost
verge of a precipitous absurdity, and the skill lies
in coming as close as possible without actually
tumbling over.'

However, it may very well be that that bright,
beautiful character, Phœbe, caused him more
trouble and thought than he was fain to acknowledge. Such is, after all, a legitimate in-
ference from what is here said. To get relief from
the sombre vein of cold and morbid analysis, seems
to have been ever his main difficulty ; and it would
almost appear as though in Phœbe—so natural, so
pure, so healthy in her devotion and self-denial—he
had resolved to create a type—the true American
woman of the time—to refute once for all the objec-
tions so loudly raised to his morbidity, and to make
an end of the remarks about his incapacity to deal
with simple and healthy life. But his own confes-

sion, here so naïvely made, is a kind of unconscious justification of the common sense of the public, which the current criticism had merely uttered in scientific terms.

Ill-health came with the finishing of this wondrous work of art. At the close of 1851 he had such an attack as indisposed him from any exertion ; and probably it was the hope of good being effected by change of air and scene, that he left Lenox and went to Concord, where he had purchased a little place to which he had given the name of the Wayside. Nothing of note was accomplished here at this time, however, save that, the moment he recovered he set about writing his 'Life of Pierce,' and gave the finishing touches to the 'Blithedale Romance,' in which we have more than anywhere else of that 'beautiful strangeness' which his imagination gave to familiar things. It may be said indeed that in 'Blithedale' Hawthorne made his genius fully efficient by 'penetrating it with passion.'

Pierce meanwhile, to the surprise of many sharp observers of American politics, had become President ; and it was not likely that he would forget his old friend and recent apologist, notwithstanding that the said old friend the first time he saw Pierce after his accession to dignity, had met him with, 'Frank, I pity you;' to which Frank had replied, with a smile, 'I pity myself.' Hawthorne was soon appointed United States Consul at Liverpool, and accordingly sailed for England in 1853.

We all know something of the prejudices and whimsical dislikes he brought to the old country with him; for he has made candid confession of all these in his work—'Our Old Home,' and in his *Note Books*. But it is very pleasing to observe how gradually familiarity vanquishes him, how he gets to love what he had been inclined to despise, and has to acknowledge himself more happy and contented on English ground than he had been for long. He found much room for observation, and could not help admiring. He loved to look on the old English manor houses, on the venerable ancient churches; nothing pleasing him more 'than a ramble through an old churchyard, reading the odd inscriptions as he went.' He acknowledges that 'of all things, I should like to find a grave-stone in one of these old churchyards with my own name upon it, although for myself I should wish to be buried in America. The graves are too horribly damp here.' His love for the old; for the shades and middle tones in which American life and history are so deficient, and which he so often desiderated, was here gratified ; and gradually he found himself so much at home that he had but little wish to leave. He found attached friends, too—of one of these, Francis Bennoch, he has spoken in such terms of love and tenderness as he used towards but few, even among his friends.

In 1858, he left Liverpool, and went to Italy. Few men have ever entered more deeply into the spirit of Italian life, notwithstanding that at first he found it difficult to strike root in Italy—feeling the change from England to the Continent as much as he had done the change from America to England, or even more. First impressions soon wore off, and he found much to engage his mind in Rome. Its art, its history, its crumbling piles of ruin, its very squalor and dirtiness, had a fascination for him. If the old Rows of Chester drew him thither over and over again, how much more must the ancient memorials of Rome have excited his interest and imagination. He was visited by affliction whilst there in the form of serious illness in his family. For relief he set himself to gather the materials for 'The Marble Faun ;' but, when his daughter was at the worst, he could do nothing. Mrs. Hawthorne informs us that for months he did not even make an entry in his note-book. We regret such omissions ; but surely facts like these add a new lustre to the character of the man who was as loving and kindly as he was greatly gifted.

His stay in Italy was very fruitful; but it is noticeable that for a long time he did not reconcile himself to the Italian schools of painting, preferring the Dutch masters, with their realism and minute details. In one point of view, indeed, Hawthorne was a realist, as is also borne out by the circumstance that, when he wrote for children, he either chose historical or biographical subjects, or contented himself with recasting classic legends.

He returned to America in the middle of 1860, and quietly re-established himself at the Wayside, Concord, for which place he had always felt a liking. He had, however, little domestic difficulties to face. Some time before he had written anticipatingly :—'If I had but a house fit to live in, I should be greatly more reconciled to going home, but I am really at a loss to imagine how we are to squeeze ourselves into that little old cottage of mine. We had outgrown it before we came away, and most of us are twice as big now as we were then.' By adding to the little cottage a sort of wing, which he dedicated to his own use, as library and so on, the

Wayside was made sufficiently roomy, and there was still promise of a peaceful and productive period of years for him. Unfortunately, his household was ere long visited with a succession of serious illnesses, which rendered it impossible for him to work steadily; then came the Civil War, in which, notwithstanding his desire to keep aloof from politics and public life, he was so deeply absorbed, that he could not retreat into solitude with the creatures of his fancy. He wrote the chapters of 'Our Old Home,' which appeared in 'The Atlantic Monthly' as he wrote them. He elaborated 'Septimius' and threw it aside again as involved and unsatisfactory to himself. Then he made a fresh start with 'Pansie' or 'The Dolliver Romance,' which he wrought at only by fits and starts, and without any sense of satisfaction, although some of the passages in this choice fragment are as felicitously turned as anything he ever wrote. He was often visited with ill-health and complete prostration both of body and mind. His elasticity and freedom seemed gone; and we find a peculiar despondency hovering over his letters from the Wayside in these years. 'Those verses entitled "Weariness" in the last magazine,' he writes to Mr. Fields, 'seem to me profoundly touching. I too am weary and begin to look ahead for the Wayside Inn.'   But there is a flicker of the old humour still : ' If I subside into the almshouse before my intellectual faculties are quite extinguished, it strikes me that I would make· a very pretty book out of it : and seriously, if I alone were concerned, I should not have any great objection to winding up there.' . . . ' You ought to be thankful that (like most other broken-down authors) I do not pester you with decrepit pages, and insist upon your accepting them as full of the old spirit and vigour. That trouble, perhaps, still awaits you, after I shall have reached a further stage of decay. Seriously, my mind has, for the present, lost its temper and its fine edge, and I have an instinct that I had better keep quiet. Perhaps I shall have a new spirit of vigour, if I wait quietly for it ; perhaps not.'

In March 1864, Hawthorne was persuaded to undertake a journey to the South for the sake of his health in the company of Mr. Ticknor. His friends at Boston all speak of the great change that had taken place in him. Without delay, the two set forth. The stronger man was taken away instead of the weakly invalid. Mr. Ticknor died suddenly at Philadelphia ; and on Hawthorne devolved the duty and the trial and grief of performing for his friend such services as he himself had expected to require at the hand of others. He returned home; but he never recovered the shock. His health rapidly gave way. Another journey to the New Hampshire Hills was undertaken in hopes of a recovery, in the company of President Pierce. Hawthorne's appearance is thus described by his friend Dr. Holmes, who saw him on this occasion as he passed through Boston. 'Late on the afternoon on the day before he left Boston, I called upon him at the hotel where he was staying. He had gone out but a moment before. Looking along the street, I saw a figure at some distance in advance which could only be his—but how changed from his former port and figure! There was no mistaking the long iron-grey locks, the carriage of the head, and the general look of the natural outlines of movement; but he seemed to have shrunken in all his dimensions, and faltered along with an uncertain, feeble step, as if every movement were an effort.'

Hawthorne died in the town of Plymouth, New Hampshire, May 19, 1864. He had often expressed a wish that he might die suddenly, and his desire was granted. 'The moment, and even the hour, could not be told, for he had passed away without giving any sign of suffering, such as might call the attention of the friend near him.' His body was taken back to Concord. 'On the summit of a gently swelling mound where the wild flowers had climbed to find the light and the stirring of fresh breezes, the tired poet was laid beneath the green turf. Poet let us call him, though his chants were not modulated in the rhythm of verse. The element of poetry is air ; we know the poet by his atmospheric effects, by the blue of his distances, by the softening of every hard outline he touches, by the silver mist in which he veils deformity and clothes what is common, so that it changes to awe-inspiring mystery, by the clouds of gold and purple which are the drapery of his dreams.'

The root of Hawthorne's genius was puritan, but he dipped the puritan sternness in finest dyes of fancy, caught largely from his early impressions. For do we not see in all his writing traces of early community with sorrow, of contact with moods most alien to childhood and youth, of the weird impression and haunting mystery of Puritan life which he drank-in during these night rambles in Salem, and plenteous evidences, too, of the deep hold which the beauty and terror of Nature had laid upon his soul in these days and nights of solitude in the Raymond woods, on the ice, or on the water? Hawthorne in one place regrets the lack of a favourable atmosphere in which the fruits of his mind might have ripened to literary form ; but yet he says of one of the most depressing periods of his life, ' I do think and feel and learn things that are worth knowing, and which I should not know unless I had learned them here, so that the present portion of my life shall not be quite left out of the sum of my real existence. . . . It is good for me, on many accounts, that my life had this passage in it.' The latter view we are inclined to think the true one. Hawthorne's debt to what seemed unfavourable circumstances is incalculable ; his life in this regard is as good an illustration as could well be found of the strange law of spiritual compensation which plays grandly through all human life, and of which he is himself, perhaps, the greatest literary exponent of later times.

Thus we can see how important to a man of Hawthorne's type was the outward life he lived, the circumstances into which he was thrown. The form of his work was to a large extent determined by these. For long periods he was often powerless, when, suddenly, a face, a figure, a defect, an odd-ness of character would give him the handle of his symbol, which for a long while he had studiously sought without any success. Often, doubtless, had Hawthorne pondered the mystery of sin, and its strange effects upon humanity, both injurious and beneficial,—even the sin of adultery had inevitably been meditated on over and over again by this most subtle casuist of human nature ; but it was not till one day, fumbling among old records, at the Custom House of Boston, he came on a sentence decreeing that a woman convicted of adultery should stand on the Meeting House steps with the letter A marked upon her breast, that the problem flashed upon his imagination in full artistic form. The friend who was beside him at the moment showed insight in saying, ' We shall hear of the letter A again.'

Another writes : ' I do not doubt but it was Thoreau's wonderful intimacies with various animals that suggested to his friend and neighbour, Mr. Hawthorne, the character of Donatello in the tale of " Transformation." ' Perhaps it may be remembered that Henry Thoreau, well-bred and well-educated, would enter none of the learned professions at the urgent wishes of his friends, but retreated into the woods, and built for himself, with

his own hands, a hut at Walden, near Concord,
where, in solitude, he pursued his studies of natural
history, with something like instinct. His love for
animals and all natural things was a passion.
Though a man of supreme brain, as is attested by
his several books and his unique letters, he was, in
his habits, really like some creature taking rank
between man and the brutes, and bringing them, as
Hawthorne feigns of Donatello and his ancestors,
into something like sympathy and good understanding. His fame spread, and he soon drew students
and children from far places.

'Sometimes,' says the writer above quoted, 'I
have gone with Thoreau and his young comrades
for an expedition on the river, to gather, it may be,
water lilies. Upon such excursions, his resources
for our entertainment were inexhaustible. He
would tell stories of the Indians who once dwelt
thereabout, until the children almost looked to see
a red man skulking with his arrow on the shore;
and every plant or flower on the bank or in the
water, and every fish, turtle, frog, lizard about us,
was transformed by the wand of his knowledge,
from the low form into which the spell of our
ignorance had reduced it, into a mystic beauty.
One of his surprises was to thrust his hand softly

into the water, and as softly raise up before our astonished eyes a large bright fish, which lay as contentedly in his hand as if they were old acquaintances. If the fish had also dropped a penny from its mouth, it could not have been a more miraculous proceeding to us. We could not then get his secret from him.'

Even then the thought of a romance, in which the chief character should unite the sylvan creatures with man in something like sympathy and mutual confidence had occurred to him. But nothing at that time came of it. He seems to have abandoned his intention, till he was in Italy, and gazed on the 'Faun of Praxiteles,' at the Villa Borghese. He then writes down his impression thus :—

'Many of the specimens of sculpture displayed in these rooms are fine, but none of them, I think, possess the highest merit. An Apollo is beautiful; a group of a fighting Amazon and her enemies trampled under her horse's feet, is very impressive; a Faun copied from that of Praxiteles and another, who seems to be dancing, were exceedingly pleasant to look at. I like these strange, sweet, playful, rustic creatures, linked so prettily, without monstrosity, to the lower tribes. . . Their character has never, that I know of, been wrought out in literature ; and something quite good, funny, and philosophical, as well as poetic, might very likely be educed from them. The Faun is a natural and delightful link betwixt human and brute life, with something of a divine character intermingled.'

Still in the same happy equable mood of mind he goes some months after, and again renews the impression derived from the Faun :—

' We afterwards went into the sculpture gallery, where I looked at the Faun of Praxiteles, and was sensible of a peculiar charm in it ; a sylvan beauty and homeliness, friendly and wild at once. The lengthened, but not preposterous ears, and the little tail, which would, we infer, have an exquisite effect, and make the spectator smile in his very heart. This race of Fauns was the most delightful of all that antiquity imagined. It seems to me that a story, with all sorts of fun and pathos in it, might be contrived on the idea of their species having become intermingled with the human race ; a family with the faun blood in them having prolonged itself from the classic era till our own days. The tail might have disappeared by dint of constant intermarriages with ordinary mortals, but the pretty hairy ears should occasionally reappear in members of the family : and the moral instincts and intellectual characteristics of the Faun might be most picturesquely brought out without detriment to the human interest in the story.'

Then nearly a month later still he again sets this down :—

' I likewise took particular note of the Faun of Praxiteles, because the idea keeps recurring to me of writing a romance about it, and, for that reason, I shall endeavour to set down a somewhat minutely itemised detail of the statue and its surroundings.'

The sight of the dead monk in the Church had evidently suggested a more tragic interest than was at first intended, and gradually the lean kine, so to say, ate up the fat ones—the simple fun and pathos were overshadowed by the tragic, the weird, and terrible. The more Hawthorne dwelt on it, the more the dead monk and the Faun inextricably interblended themselves, and refused to be separated ; suggesting themselves as symbols for an artistic statement of the manner in which sin may stimulate the hitherto dormant moral powers. And it was always so, more or less, with him. Naturally good-tempered, hopeful, sunshiny, he had not the power to ' write a sunshiny book,' though he often expressed the wish that he had. Before he left England, he wrote : " When I get home, I will try

and write a more genial book ; but the Devil himself always seems to get into my inkstand, and I
can only exorcise him by pensful at a time.' He
could not write till he was haunted by some
weird idea—till he had stirred up some thought
that lay almost at the unallowed recesses of his
nature, so that he had to peer down into the
depths to see how it muddied the waters—catching glimpses of the shadow of his own face between
whiles.

With that peculiar power of abstracting himself,
as it were, from his own intellectual activity, he sets
down in the calmest manner how his stories took
shapes which he himself had not at first designed,
and recognises himself as being, in fact, a 'haunted
man.' And so he really was. His mind, by its
very nature, was constantly hovering over the
boundary that divides sense from spirit ; and hence
the strange ghostliness that sometimes haunts one
in reading him. But the reader is haunted simply
because Hawthorne himself was haunted, and could
only escape by taking to retirement and writing
down the results of his self-observations. He was
a haunted man, who craved contact with men and
the world to quicken the imagination and make it
fix on some one point ; and this being once attained,

he then needed absolute retirement till the work was done.

It is noticeable that after the conception of 'The Marble Faun' had come to something like clearness in his mind, he then sought absolute solitude, notwithstanding that he was still in Italy, amidst its many sights and scenes, its clear air, and stately architecture, and gorgeous paintings. 'Six months of uninterrupted monotony would be more valuable to me just now, than the most brilliant succession of novelties,' is his singular confession. But when he had once written out his conception, the need for contact with the real world returned in double force. This necessity, indeed, was what saved him. He would have been simply melancholic and help-less, if it had not been a necessity of his nature that he should go out and observe; that he re-mained literally unproductive until he had caught from real life at once the impulse to production and the symbol with which to work. The ex-haustive verification of this fact would form one of the most interesting of literary exercises. It is worth a moment's trouble. If we get a clear idea of Hawthorne's dependence on reality and the world without, and the effect it had on his whole develop-ment, it may turn out a not unfruitful bit of work.

Mr. Moncure Conway, who has written a very
graceful little sketch of Hawthorne for Mr. Hot-
ten's edition of the ' American Note-Books,' takes
occasion to say that, ' No one who has been startled
by seeing the strange profile on the side of the
Profile Mountains in New Hampshire, can doubt
where the story of "The Great Stone Face" was con-
ceived.' But in 1840 we find Hawthorne recording
in his Note-book what is evidently the original
suggestion for this story, which does not seem to
acknowledge any such specific local reference,
though no doubt the Profile Mountain brought the
idea into definite objective form at the last. ' The
semblance of a human face to be formed on the
side of a mountain, or in the fracture of a small
stone, by a *lusus naturæ*. The face is an object of
curiosity for years or centuries ; by-and-by a boy
is born, whose features gradually assume the aspect
of that portrait. At some critical juncture the resemblance is found to be perfect. A prophecy
might be connected.' Even the phantasy of self-
criticism, which is so humorously carried out by
way of introducing the wonderful tale of ' Rappac-
cini's Daughter,' was evidently suggested by the
circumstances of the queer little foreigner, half
Swiss, half German, whom Hawthorne met in

1837, at Bridge's on the Kennebec, and who Frenchified Hawthorne's name into M. de l'Aubé-pine.

The more closely we enquire, the more definitely we can fix the starting-points of fact and incident on which he built his unique creations. Perhaps the story of 'The Great Carbuncle' affords the most remarkable illustration of this. A sketch, which until now has not been published in this country, throws a veritable flood of light on his process of creation. We discover that, in the story, we have but a set of real circumstances lifted into a sort of misty atmosphere of allegorical meaning, the moral purport shining powerfully through, and imparting to the whole a peculiar dusky brightness. By comparing this 'Notch of the White Mountains' with the allegory point by point, all this will the better be brought out. The characters, one by one, we can identify: the very dress and features of the folks he met at Ethan Crawford's mountain hostel are reproduced for us in a different atmosphere. 'One was a mineralo-gist, a scientific, green-spectacled figure in black, bearing a heavy hammer, with which he did great damage to the precipices and put the fragments in his pockets. . . . I asked the mineralogist whether, in his researches about these parts, he had found the three "Silver Hills," which an Indian Sachem sold to an Englishman nearly two hundred years ago, and the treasure of which the posterity of the purchaser have been looking for ever since. But the man of science had ransacked every hill along the Saco, and knew nothing of the prodigious piles of wealth.' Now, behold the identical figure thrown into the magnifying atmosphere of allegory : 'The fourth of the group had no name that his companions knew of, and was chiefly distinguished by a sneer that always contorted his thin visage, and by a prodigious pair of spectacles, which were supposed to deform and discolour the whole face of nature to this gentleman's perception. . . . These coloured spectacles probably darkened the cynic's sight, in at least as great a degree as the smoked glasses through which people gaze on an eclipse. . . . "The Great Carbuncle," cried the cynic, with ineffable scorn, "Why, you blockhead, there is no such thing in *rerum naturâ*. I have come three thousand miles, and am resolved to set my foot on every peak of these mountains, and poke my head in every chasm, for the sole purpose of demonstrating, to the satisfaction of any man that the "Great Carbuncle" is a humbug.'

Here, too, we have the actual poet : ' Another was a well-dressed young man, who carried an opera-glass set in gold, and seemed to be making a quotation from some of Byron's rhapsodies on mountain scenery.'   Afterwards, inside the hotel, we are told that ' two Georgians present held the album between them, and favoured us with the few specimens of its contents, which they considered ridiculous enough to be worth hearing.   One extract met with deserved applause.   It was a " Sonnet to the Snow on Mount Washington," and had been contributed that very afternoon, bearing a signature of great distinction in magazines and annuals. The lines were elegant and full of fancy, but too remote from familiar sentiment and cold as their subject, resembling those curious specimens of crystallised vapour which I observed next day on the mountain-top.   The poet was understood to be the young gentleman of the opera-glass, who heard our laudatory remarks with the composure of a veteran.'   Then this is the idealised poet : ' The fifth adventurer likewise lacked a name, which was the greater pity, as he appeared to be a poet.   He was a bright-eyed man who wofully pined away, which was no more than natural, if, as some people affirmed, his ordinary diet was fog, morning mist, and a slice of the densest cloud within his reach, sauced with moon-shine whenever he could get it.'

Then there is a physician, the original of Doctor Cacaphodel; and a 'trader from Burlington, and an old squire of the Green Mountains; and two young married couples all the way from Massachusetts, on the matrimonial jaunt. Besides these strangers, the rugged country of Coos, in which we were, was represented by half-a-dozen wood-cutters who had slain a bear in the forest and smitten off his paw.' So here we see the whole of the raw material of the 'Great Carbuncle,' and its parts are still identifiable after its wonderful transmogrification. Even the most delicate touch about the young couple retiring to the corner, the bride having contrived to erect a little curtain to screen themselves from the rest, is substantially a reproduction. 'The two brides and the doctor's wife held a whispered discussion, which, by their frequent titterings and a blush or two, seemed to have reference to the trials or enjoyments of the matrimonial state. The bridegrooms sat together in a corner, rigidly silent, like Quakers whom the spirit moveth not, being still in the odd predicament of bashfulness towards their own young wives.'

Mr. Fields tells us that, when a youth, Hawthorne made a journey into New Hampshire with his uncle, Samuel Manning. They travelled in a two-wheeled chaise, and met with many adventures which the young man chronicled in his home letters. Some of the touches in these epistles were very characteristic and amusing, and showed in these early years his quick observation and descriptive power. The travellers 'put up' at Farmington, in order to rest over Sunday. Hawthorne writes to a member of the family in Salem : 'As we were wearied with rapid travelling, we found it impossible to attend divine service, which was, of course, very grievous to us both. In the evening, however, I went to a bible-class with a very polite and agreeable gentleman, whom I afterwards discovered to be a strolling tailor, of very questionable habits.'

When the travellers arrived at the Shaker village of Canterbury, Hawthorne at once made the acquaintance of the Community there, and the account which he sent home was to the effect that the brothers and sisters led a good and comfortable life, and he wrote : 'If it were not for the ridiculous ceremonies, a man might do worse than join them.' Indeed, he spoke to them about becoming a member of the Society, and was evidently impressed with the thrift and peace of the establishment. This visit in early life to the Shakers is interesting as suggesting to Hawthorne his beautiful story of 'The Canterbury Pilgrims,' which is in his volume of 'The Snow Image' and other 'Twice Told Tales.'

Such facts as these give us some insight into Hawthorne's manner of working. He burrowed, to use his own phrase, 'to the utmost of his ability, into the depths of our common nature for the purposes of psychological romance;' but it was essential to him that, before casting any thought into artistic form, he should receive from real life at least the handle of his symbol. Very little often sufficed him for this, but it was a *conditio sine quâ non* that he should have that little, if he was to be in any degree effective. Even 'The Minister's Veil' is but a new allegorical rendering of the sad fate of Mr. Moody of Maine. This Hawthorne himself has freely acknowledged. To a number of his stories he at first attached notes, acknowledging the real facts on which he raised his airy fabric of allegory. And certainly it is surpassingly noteworthy that in the earlier 'American Note-books' we find Hawthorne more employed in 'burrowing' inward for principles, than in seeking for symbols in the outside world ; while in the 'English Note-books' the process is exactly reversed. He no longer thinks it worth while to busy himself with setting down records of his subjective phantasies, but is rather curious and active to fix traits, characters, and incidents, suitable for being transformed into symbols. And just as the wisdom of the fancy became more and more the real possession of the intellect and the heart, he seems to have less cared for the perplexing joys of solitude, and learned to feel more relief and pleasure from contact with his fellow-men. Thus, it seems to us, that Mrs. Hawthorne's words, prefatory to these 'English Note-books,' apply with much more force to the American ones. She writes :

'Throughout his journals it will be seen that Mr. Hawthorne is *entertaining*, and not *asserting*, opinions and ideas. He questions, doubts, and reflects with his pen, and as it were, instructs himself. So that these Note-books should be read, not as definite conclusions of his mind, but often merely as passing impressions. Whatever *conclusions* he arrived at are condensed in the works given to the world by his own hand, in which will never be found a careless word.'

Had we more space at our command, we believe
it would be easy to verify this statement by extracts. We must give one or two :—

'The dying exclamation of the Emperor Au-
gustus. Has it not been well acted? An essay
on the misery of being always under a mask. A
veil may be needed, but never a mask.'

Under date 1837, we find these records :—

'A blind man to set forth on a walk through
ways unknown to him, and to trust to the guidance
of anybody who will take the trouble ; the different characters who would undertake it ; some mis-
chievous, some well-meaning, but incapable ; perhaps one blind man undertakes to lead another.
At last, possibly he rejects all guidance, and blun-
ders on by himself.'

'A person to be in possession of something, as
perfect as mortal man has a right to demand ; he
tries to make it better, and ruins it entirely.' [This
is an idea which occurs under various refinements.
Thus we have it some years later] : 'A person to
be the death of his beloved in trying to raise her
to more than mortal perfection, yet his aiming so
highly should be a comfort to him.'

'Some very famous jewel or other thing, much
talked of over the world. Some person to meet

with it, and get possession of it in some unexpected manner, amid homely circumstances.'

' A woman to sympathise with all emotions, yet to have none of her own.'

In one of his earliest Note-books we find him questioning the effect which the slaying of a fellow-creature, in circumstances such as made the act in some sense innocent, would have upon a brooding and speculative character, sensitive, and every way more inclined to thought and scepticism than to action or belief. The suggestion frequently, and in varied forms, recurs to him ; and no doubt the recollection of the lad who, according to tradition, slew the wounded soldier with the axe, near the Old Manse, had its own share in keeping the subject before his mind. How, at last, he did work out such a theme, with what subtlety, delicacy, and variety of *motif*, English readers can now see in his latest novel—' Septimius.' All that seems rude or contradictory in the tradition is refined away ;—Septimius is a student, stricken with a sense of the mystery of life and immortality. Out of his love for Rose Garfield—as yet untestified in words—rises the passion that made him hate, before the circumstances came that made him kill, the gay young officer ; and, through the slaying of a creature whose sunshiny good-nature and generosity had already called forth his affection, in spite of his first desire for revenge, he obtains that wonderful document which has such a profound influence on his fate. Truly, the story told by Lowell over the nameless grave of the two British soldiers was anything but lost. The subtle workings of Hawthorne's mind upon it, as it lay there for many years, has transformed it into one of the subtlest revelations of the workings of the human soul. Notwithstanding that the plan never clearly developed itself in Hawthorne's mind ; and that, at the middle of the story, as we have it, he changed his purpose with respect to the relations of Rose and Septimius ; yet we can see what a masterpiece of art he could have made of it, had his health been better, and had he been a little while longer spared.

The peculiarly abstract character of his earlier conceptions is what most strikes one. They are so utterly without any apparent reference to the real world, and suggest only the vaguest moral paradoxes. The following, however, is of a somewhat different kind, and on the whole is more of the character of remark we meet with in the English Note-books.

' The other day, at the entrance of the market-house, I saw a woman sittting in a small hand-waggon, apparently for the purpose of receiving alms. There was no attendant at hand ; but I noticed that one or two persons who passed by seemed to enquire whether she wished her waggon to be moved. Perhaps this is her mode of making progress about the city, by the voluntary aid of boys and other people who help to drag her. There is something in this—I don't yet well know what—that has impressed me, as if I could make a romance out of the idea of a woman living in this manner a public life, and moving about by such means.'

When one begins a systematic study of Haw-thorne—eager to get all the light that circumstances can throw upon his strange creations—the Note-books, interesting in themselves, become very tan-talising and unsatisfactory. They are so broken and disconnected. They jump from epoch to epoch, leaving some of the most interesting periods wholly dark. Thus, in the American Note-books, we have no record of the all-important years be-tween 1825 and 1835, when 'The Twice Told Tales' were written, and when the most decisive in-fluences were at work in forming Hawthorne's character ; the year spent at Boston, as weigher and gauger under Bancroft, is summed up in a dozen pages of extracts from his letters ; the period of the surveyorship at Salem, extending over three years, has no record here at all, nor has the time he remained at Salem, after his escape from the Custom-house, before he went to Lenox in 1850. Yet all these periods are biographically interesting —that the first is especially so is clear from the very significant glance which he casts backwards, and which gives the passage a good right to be here presented, although it appears in the English Note-books in 1856 :—

'I think I have been happier this Christmas than ever before by my own fireside, and with my wife and children about me—more content to enjoy what I have—less anxious for anything beyond it in this life. My early life was, perhaps, a good preparation for the declining half of life ; it having been such a blank that any thereafter would com- pare favourably with it. For a long, long while, I have occasionally been visited with a singular dream ; and I have an impression that I have dreamt it ever since I have been in England. It is, that I am still at college—or sometimes even at school—and there is a sense that I have been there unconscionably long, and have quite failed to make such progress as my contemporaries have done; and I seem to meet some of them with a feeling of shame and depression that broods over me as I think of it, even when awake. *This dream, recurring all through these twenty or thirty years, must be one of the effects of that heavy seclusion in which I shut myself up for twelve years after leaving college, when everybody moved onward, and left me behind. How strange that it should come now, when I may call myself famous and prosperous—when I am happy too!'*

Mrs. Hawthorne, indeed, tells us in her preface, that as no journals were found prior to those of 1835, Mr. Hawthorne must have destroyed those he had written, which is a circumstance ever to be regretted. Had the wide gaps only been filled up, we should have had something like a complete and wholly unconscious memoir from Hawthorne's own hand. As it is, we sometimes feel a little vexed that Mrs. Hawthorne has defrauded us of details of close personal interest, and has too often added to the wrong by irritating us with asterisks. It was not Hawthorne's way to reveal too much even to his own eye; he was ever watchful over his confessions to himself. 'I have often felt,' he writes, 'that words may be a thick and darksome veil between the soul and the truth which it seeks. Wretched were we, indeed, if we had no better means of communicating ourselves, no fairer garb in which to array our essential being, than these poor rags and tatters of Babel!' But that is only a reason, why, if we are to be let into such a man's confidence at all, we should receive it wholly and not partially. Just when we fancy we are to be drawn into a somewhat closer confidence, the Rhadamanthine hand of the editor is put forward and pulls our companion aside. But perhaps we are inclined to fancy that more was thus kept from us than really has been so. Anyway, to the end we feel that there is much untold, and that even now we are somewhat in the position of the old Quaker, who wrote to Hawthorne, ' that he had been reading my introduction to the " Mosses " and " The Scarlet Letter," and felt as if he knew me better than his best friend,' which only calls forth from Hawthorne the quietly incisive words: ' But I think he considerably over-estimates the extent of his intimacy with me.' We must not fall into the old Quaker's error, and over-estimate the extent of our intimacy with him.

But to those in quest of characteristics, the Note-books cannot fail to be, in the highest sense, attractive. All Hawthorne's prejudices, whims, and strange fancies find frankest revelation on the page, and in a style that radiates ever and anon all the peculiar fascination of his singular mind. He had left orders that no formal life of him should be given to the world; and his wife, believing that she was free to communicate as much of his private notes as could be thrown into form, thus discovered a means of gratifying a not unnatural curiosity on the part of a large section of readers, and, at the same time, of conforming with her late husband's wish. We are not sure but Hawthorne is as directly revealed by this means as he could have been in any other way. One of his characters, he says, made himself awful only by hiding his face; and a good deal of the mystery that is inseparable from a man of Hawthorne's type is his perpetual attempt to escape from himself in the very telling of his story through the veil of abnormal characters or conditions.

His mind was eminently of the elusive kind. Let him be as communicative and confidential as he may, he still keeps something back, acting, as it would seem, on the short counsel of the Scotch poet—

But still keep something to yersel'
Ye scarcely tell to ony.

It consisted with the very nature of the man so to do. He was almost as much a puzzle to himself as he was to anyone else. He seemed, in fact, to be two men; and the one was constantly in the attitude of watching and commenting on the other. Hence the lyrical quality of his writing, and yet what he has called its 'objectivity'—the power of suddenly veiling his own moods and impressions, and giving them the aspect of being something foreign, simply by dint of setting them faithfully alongside of other and alien moods, which he treats with equal impartiality. From this arises what appears his inquisitorial curiosity, but this, after all, consisted rather in a desire to analyse himself than to spy upon others—to trace the impressions— shadowy as the wind-waves passing over the wheat in autumn—on his own delicate nature, and in some sense to fix and perpetuate them.

All his works are thus biographies of moods and experiences; only he needs the spectrum of other and alien moods through which to exhibit them. The peculiarly subtle manner in which he involves himself with the most morbid and conflicting of human emotions is, to a large extent, the secret of his strange attractiveness. And of this he himself seems to have been quite conscious; for we find him thus writing in the dedication of his 'Snow Image' to his friend Horatius Bridge :—

'There is no harm, but on the contrary, good, in arranging some of the ordinary facts of life in a slightly idealised and artistic guise. *I have taken facts which relate to myself, because they chance to be nearest at hand, and likewise are my own property.* And as for egotism, a person who has been burrowing, to the utmost of his ability, into the depths of our common nature, for the purposes of psychological romance, and who pursues his researches in that dusky region, as he needs must, as well by the tact of sympathy as the light of observation, will smile at incurring such an imputation in virtue of a little preliminary talk about his external habits, his abode, his casual associates, and other matters entirely upon the surface. *These things hide the man instead of displaying him. You must make quite another kind of inquest, and look through the whole range of his fictitious characters, good and evil, in order to detect any of his essential traits.'*

A history of Hawthorne's inner life, as he himself confesses, thus lay in solution in his stories. He uniformly took facts which related to himself, because they chanced to be nearest at hand, and likewise were his own property. A satisfactory biography of him would thus, on one side, have been as nearly as possible an analysis of his books, and an attempt to discover the real and substantial groundwork in each of them. Perhaps this was the reason why Hawthorne was so determined that no one should undertake a life. He himself only could write a life, and he had already written it so far, in the only way in which it could be satisfactorily written. His life distributes itself into cycles, each one being marked by a crisis—the casting off of the shell of an old experience, and the appropriation of the new one, being signalised by the advent of a book. For ' men of uncommon intellect, who have grown morbid, possess this occasional power of mighty effort, into which they throw the life of many days, and then are lifeless for as many more.' It is very remarkable that, while he complains of the stagnation of his productive faculties during his employment at Salem Custom House and other places, he then seemed, nevertheless, to be quite consciously appropriating the needful material to be sooner or later drawn out in the shining webs of romance. And these ' periods of suspended animation ' seemed as much a necessity of his genius as were the favourable circumstances for production. His life was a perpetual series of reactions, in which what we may call the two selves took position to view each other. 'Though my form be absent, my inner man goes constantly to church.' Hawthorne's inner man, indeed, went into many places from which the form was absent ; and the special characteristic of his genius is that he never failed to look back upon the other self left behind as being something shadowy, dreamlike, unreal. He believes only in his own mental world : men and outer things only *begin* to have a real existence for him, when they glide from out their ordinary relations to interpret and reveal that wonderful inner life of his. Men are but shadows drawn sometimes by a sort of fascination across the glass-slide of his imagination, leaving their impress there ; but they are absolutely dim and colourless, if not viewed at proper distance and in congenial lights. Says the showman of Main Street, no other than Hawthorne himself, idealising history for us : 'Only oblige me by standing further back, and, take my word for it, the slips of pasteboard shall assume spiritual life, and the bedaubed canvas become an airy and changeable reflex of what it purports to represent.'

There are some writers who lead you with them by the hand into the very midst of the scene they portray—pointing out the characters of note, and introducing you, one by one, to those their familiars, thus helping you gradually to take in the whole scene from different points of view, and who thus excel, by the very want of atmosphere and the magic relief of subtle shades and side-tints. They scarcely put anything in words which a painter of ordinary capability would not creditably paint, or, at all events, paint in such a way that you would not be instantly shocked with a sense of disharmony and impropriety. But Hawthorne is of a very different order. Every fresh condition that appeals to his sympathy sufficiently to lead him to seek in the most remote way to *dramatically* involve himself with it, is but a new magic circle into which he may transport himself to look thence upon real life, and eject over it a dewy haze as of morning mist, yet so changing the whole aspects and relations of things as to be a veil of mystery, wonder, and surprise. But he never for a moment loses the overpowering consciousness that he has but transported *one* self there, to be wistfully viewed and contemplated by another self, hidden away among the shadows and foliage, and sometimes among rocks, such as those where Love was fabled of the ancients to dwell. It is this wistful selfdividedness, which, in our opinion, is the key to Hawthorne's character, and the mysterious nearness yet far-offness of his art.

Hawthorne, in one place, significantly likened himself to a '*doppel-ganger*,' and that essentially expresses the leading elements of his character. It is a radical mistake to suppose that, because he loved solitude, he was withdrawn from life and its manifold interests. No man ever had a keener or more watchfully anxious curiosity respecting all that concerns man, all that is bound up in the possibilities of human nature. These confessions are characteristically true :—

'Though fond of society, I was so constituted as to need occasional retirements, even in a life like that of *Blithedale*, which was itself characterised by remoteness from the world. Unless renewed by a yet further withdrawal towards the inner circle of self-communion, I lost the better part of my individuality. My thoughts became of little worth, and my sensibilities grew as arid as a tuft of moss (a thing whose life is in the shade, the rain, or the noontide dew), crumbling in the sunshine, after long expectance of a shower.'

And yet elsewhere in the same work he confesses that—

'No sagacious man will long retain his sagacity if he live exclusively among reformers and progressive people, *without periodically returning into the settled system of things, to correct himself by a new observation from that old standpoint.*'

Thus it comes about that, while the inner life of Hawthorne seems at first to be the all-important thing in a study of his writings, we find, before we have proceeded far, that in few cases has a great writer been more dependent on outer circumstances for giving the impulse to production, and determining the form and pattern of it. Fulfilling, so to speak, in his inner life and imagination, all possible abnormal experiences and composite conditions of feeling, even at times verging upon the inhuman, he approaches life, not so much as an artist, as a scientific man. He is desirous rather of verifying his own fancies, than of broadly and sympathetically viewing life to represent it as it is. Hence arises the 'coldness' which, as he himself remarks, is inseparable from the most effective portions of his work. You cannot 'take it into the mind without a shiver,' he goes on to say. This, to a great extent, proceeds from the conscious and determinate ends with which he approached the real world. He was incessantly on the outlook for symbols by which fitly to declare himself. The world was, to a large extent, another Egyptian gallery, from whose strange and motley groups he desired to isolate a figure or hieroglyph here and there, to testify for ever to his marvellous depth of thought and penetration of the paradoxes of human life. He often tried to overcome this tendency in his character, but without result. He must either be a silent hypochondriac, or he must go out and mingle observant in the busy stream of destiny that courses through all active human life. Repelled from men by the innate shyness of his nature, he was ever drawn to them by that triumphant need of utterance which betrays the artist. He was blamed for abusing confidences when he painted his brethren of Salem Custom-House, and so he was when he pourtrayed the community of Brooke Farm; yet he is absolutely right in the excuse he urged, that he had no personal interest in the representations. To him they were merely serviceable as supplying suggestions of masks or symbols for great spiritual realities.

'Nor,' he argues, 'are these present pages a bit of intrusive biography. Let not the reader wrong me by supposing it. I never should have written with half such unreserve, had it been a portion of this life congenial to my nature, which I am living now, instead of a series of incidents and characters *entirely apart from my own concerns, and on which the qualities, personally proper to me, could have had no bearing.'*

In a certain sense, indeed, Hawthorne never realised the practical nearness of anything, save what identified itself closely with his deepest affections. The officials of the custom-house of Salem were as remote from him as though they had belonged to a community in the moon. He would have written of both with equally unconscious freedom. For individual men he cares not, unless he has been led to love them ; in *man*, he is deeply interested : but it is in a curious and remotely speculative way. Indeed, it may be said, that he has no direct concern with character as such, character is to him rather a ready medium through which to pour the stream of his own phantasies.

He needed solitude ; he needed society ; he re-presents Coverdale as escaping from Blithedale to the city, to spy on people at their back-doors. He disliked the *finesse* of society and all its make-believes ; and yet he acknowledges his liking to study the physiognomy of cities, to pry into all their crannies and out-of-the-way corners. But it needed to be at a certain distance, so that he could isolate and arrange what he saw to suit his own fancy. Too close contact often spoiled the illusion : for then his heart spoke, and the person was transformed into a portion of his own life ; and its secret was a confidence. Hence we can well believe what Mrs. Hawthorne has said : 'He had the power of putting himself into each person's situation, and of looking from every point of view, which made his charity most comprehensive. From this cause he necessarily attracted confidences, and became confessor to many sinning and suffering souls, to whom he gave tender sympathy and help, while resigning judgment to the Omnipotent and All-wise.' In spite of his 'awful insight' he was as blind as a child to the defects of his friends. As we have found, he could see nothing to blame in his old college-mate, Franklin Pierce. He has given no portrait of a confessed friend in his fiction. Indeed, nearness to him blinded him. He felt that the extension of the realm of the heart by new individual affections narrowed the range of his observing power. Therefore he was jealous of making new friends : to them he literally gave away, far more than most men, a part of himself,— of his own creative faculty. Whenever he got interested in a character, so as to love it, he could no more analyse or dissect it for his artistic uses; and hence the cold reserve in which he oftentimes seemed to wrap himself. Coverdale, in 'Blithedale,' says significantly with respect to the Hermitage : ' I brought thither no guest, *because, after Hollingsworth failed me, there was no longer the man alive with whom I could think of sharing all. So there I used to sit, owl-like, yet not without liberal and hospitable thoughts.* I counted the innumerable clusters of my vine, and forereckoned the abundance of my vintage. It gladdened me to anticipate the surprise of the community, when, like an allegorical figure of rich October, I should make my appearance, with shoulders bent beneath the burden of rich grapes, and some of the crushed ones crimsoning my brow as with a blood-stain.' His genius constantly masters him. He has always more power in depicting what is repellent to his intellectual and moral sense than what he can personally love and admire. His ' Life of Pierce ' is forced in spite of the love which he bore the man ; but Hollingsworth, whom he dislikes, is characterised by the most distinctive and incisive points of portraiture.

Nor could anything well be more characteristic

than the account he gives of his meeting with Douglas Jerrold,—how the little man was shocked that Hawthorne should think of him as a hard, 'acrid,' cynical creature, how the tears actually came into his eyes at being so misunderstood, and how Hawthorne, even while he felt there was a good deal of acting in the whole thing, could not help letting Jerrold creep into a corner of his heart. The note-books are full of direct instances of this— notably so is the record of the Englishwoman who came to him and said she was an American, and 'fooled him out of half-a-crown, which, after all, he might have spent in a far worse way.'

Hence there is some ground for saying, as indeed Zenobia did say of Miles Coverdale, that a shrinking sensitiveness, almost maiden-like, was combined in Hawthorne, with a cold curiosity truly Yankee-like. Zenobia had long recognised Coverdale 'as a sort of transcendental Yankee, with all the propensity of your countrymen to investigate matters that come within your range, but rendered almost poetical in your case by refined methods which you adopt for its gratification.'

The 'cold curiosity' of Hawthorne, however, must not be spoken of as though it were absolute and all pervasive. He was saved from the worst result of

this temper, as we have said, by warm human attach-
ments which, rendering him blind even to the most
patent faults of his favourites, restored his faith.
He owed more to his blindness than to his insight,
and he himself would doubtless have said that we
all do. He was no sceptic. He believed in God
and in humanity, with a firm and unquestioning
allegiance. Only he was a keen detector of the
false coin of humanity, and needed to protect himself against the scorn and cynicism which that qua-
lification necessarily tends to engender. His heart
was simple, though his intellect was large and keen.
Indeed we discover now and again a trace of self-
hate, when his suspicions carry him into too pro-
nounced attitudes of dislike. If he quickly detects
the bad side of any creature, he must for his own
peace pursue the investigation until he finds some
justifying trait or disposition. Nothing is so bad
but it may have its use ; no creature is so debased
but he may be a minister of good. And this is
carried so far with him indeed, that, while reading
him, we are constantly forced into a sort of questioning as to whether there is such a thing as evil
after all, and whether we ever can tell, amid the
mixed and most fluctuating elements of life, what
is for the good of the individual or of the race

And yet there is a peculiar shadow lying at the root of his optimism. In the 'New Adam and Eve,' he says, 'There must have been shadows enough, even amid the primal sunshine of their existence, to suggest the thought of the soul's incongruity with its circumstances.'

But the larger sphere which the soul inevitably seeks must finally be found, as it only can be found, in Love; and, firmly believing this, Hawthorne is only cynical for a moment; and then he seems to reprove himself even for the momentary mood. Hence there is what we should hardly have expected to find in such a man—a dominating cheerfulness.   Unless we have realised this, it is somewhat puzzling at first to find him, in 1856, writing thus :—'I have suffered wofully from low spirits for some time past; and *this has not often been the case since I grew to be a man, even in the least auspicious periods of my life.*'

We should have fancied that Hawthorne was one of the most despondent of men. But when we find that there was such a large sphere of his nature kept wholly intact from all the confusion that may be bred of psychological riddle-reading—a pure chamber of love and trust—we at once find the sufficient explanation. Otherwise it is hardly possible that the 'cold observer' could have written thus :—

'I am glad to think that God sees through my heart ; and, if any angel has power to penetrate into it, he is welcome to know everything that is there. Yes ; and so may any mortal who is capable of full sympathy, and, therefore, worthy to come into my depths. But he must find his own way there. I can neither guide nor enlighten him. It is this involuntary reserve, I suppose, that has given the objectivity to my writings ; and when people think that I am pouring myself out in a tale or an essay, I am merely telling what is common to human nature, not what is peculiar to myself. I sympathise with them, not they with me.'

And how shall we fitly characterise the massive product of this most subtle mind ? As the essence of his genius was Puritan, we may say that his novels are properly the poetry of Puritan sentiment. Take from them the almost bloodless spirituality, which sprang from his early contact with the terrible problems of sin and death and the future, and all interest would vanish. 'Strong traits of his rugged ancestors,' he frankly acknowledges, 'had intertwined themselves with his,' although he was but a 'frivolous writer of story-books.' To him as to them there is but one reality—Eternity. So close does it lie to his constant thought, that nothing more frequently occurs in his writings than questionings as to whether the real world is not more shadowy after all than the spiritual one. One of his characters in making this declaration is, for the moment, but Hawthorne's own mouthpiece : ' More and more I recognise that we dwell in a world of shadows ; and, for my part, I hold it hardly worth the trouble to attempt a distinction between shadows in the mind and shadows out of it. If there be any difference, the former are rather the more substantial.' The pervading ghostliness of his conceptions springs from the intensity with which this was constantly felt. His characters are the embodied passions, emotions, yearnings, and hopes of human nature. A cold current of ghostliness comes near us with their presence. They are just as much clothed on with flesh and blood as to render them visible to us. We see them for an instant, while we remain fixed in the position in which the Master has been pleased to place us— the moment we move to get a fuller or a closer view, they vanish from our sight. This strangely elusive quality of Hawthorne's characters is very

notable ; and still more the skill with which he nevertheless manages, by the play of peculiar lights of
fancy, to give relief and variety to his singularly airy
abstractions. 'Gradually individual beings, definite
in spiritual quality, but shadowy in substantial
form, group themselves around his central conceptions, and assume an outward body and expression
corresponding to the internal nature.'[1] To him
there are still demons and witches and angels, but
they are more closely identified with the large facts
of human nature than heretofore. In man's life
itself all the weird conceptions of man seem to be
secretly realised, if we could but read it truly.
And the laws of the spiritual world, secret, subtle,
irresistible cannot be baulked. They alone are
permanently powerful ; and justify themselves in
the last result of all. Other things are but appear-
ances and delusions that draw men to destruction.

But the element of faith in Hawthorne, though
in one point of view a product of the Puritan influence, is associated with peculiar fatalistic tendencies, owing to the hesitant wistful nature of his
genius, exaggerated, as it was, by generous contact

[1] Mr. Edwin P. Whipple's 'Character and Characteristic Men,'
p. 236 (Boston : Osgood & Co., 1870). A work of rare insight and
subtlety.

with all the culture of his time. He would not persecute for any cause, as did his ancestors; but this is only because he sees far more clearly than they did, that wrong-doing and falseness of all kinds infallibly carry their own punishment with them—a punishment which is far more terrible than any form of physical pain could possibly be. The passivity of his nature accords with his convictions; but still he is strong in his sense of justice, sometimes even to the point of cruelty, as his forefathers were. He, like them, can punish severely, although he uniformly takes care that Providence and the inner nature shall combine to effect the punishment. But with him punishment is purification. He can therefore sometimes deal out very hard measure even to those whom he seems to like; for this is the form in which the idea of atonement figures itself in his mind. He will not favour any ' poetic justice:' poor Hepzibah Pyncheon, unloved yet most worthy to be loved, in her extreme sensitiveness to the scorn of her customers, suffers for some of the sins of her scheming ancestors; and Zenobia, in ' Blithedale,' so strong and self-sufficing, must go down at last, as if under a dark wave of Fate.

The Puritan theology taught that we are not, and

cannot be, saved by any goodness of our own, that of ourselves we are only evil—tainted with sin from the birth; that we are the sorrowful victims of morbid inheritances, of the strange fatalities of constitutional depravity; and that it is only through the imputation of another's righteousness that we can hope for salvation. So far, it is thus also in Hawthorne's scheme of things. He believes in inherited evils—in defects of will, in taints of blood, in diabolic tendencies of nature; but he has firm faith also in a divine purpose which embraces human life, and turns what appears to be only evil to the individual, into good for the Whole, in which he is finally embraced. We atone for each other by turns; and if not willingly, then Providence is avenger, and 'wrongs the wronger till he render right.'

Had Hawthorne been as sceptical of Providence as he was of men he would have been helplessly melancholy. He could never have looked into other men with the steady quietness that he did, and his tales had been simply oppressive, if it had not been for this ever-present background of faith in humanity and its possibilities. Humanity is on the way towards a higher condition, and each individual, *will he, nil he,* must contribute his quota of help. But let no man trust in himself in view of the higher ends of life. Here we find the nexus between his highest speculative principles and his political and practical ideas. He is a fatalistic optimist, preaching his doctrine with the weapons of the romancer. A touch of cynicism comes in whenever he regards individuals aiming to grasp and appropriate to themselves a secret which is the right of all; for he sees no hope for persons as such. 'The world will be more and more;' but the best directed efforts of the most far-sighted men, are as likely to hinder as to promote that end. They, indeed, are quacks who make it their aim to overreach or to outrun Providence, even in struggling for ends the very noblest. For the moment that a man is impatient of a high result, and struggles or fights for it, he has lost faith and has become only ambitious; and ambition is always, and in all its forms, a cruel slave-driver. Compulsion is of its very essence. This is as much the case when the *object* seems noble as when it is mean. Philanthropy—become a mere profession or an all-absorbing purpose,—a Moloch to which sweet human affections must be daily offered up,—is as vain and is likely to be almost as fruitful of evil result as is wickedness itself. Hawthorne sometimes winks with the eye that is fixed on the follies and delusions of the individual; he never winks with the eye that is directed to the spiritual world. This completely saves him from cynicism. All his insight never robbed him of his faith in that, but confirmed it. We have already quoted a passage which proves how true a spiritualist he was; and yet how he hates the 'spiritualists,' and holds them up to ridicule. In one word, Hawthorne holds by Providence, and not by men. Yet his idea, too boldly stated, would tend to paralyse noble effort. For this we blame him. Providence needs its human agents; but, amidst the materialism and the self-faith and the pretence of the present century, was it not something to hear a clear voice like that of Hawthorne raised in favour of other influences than those which men may put forth on their own account?

Hawthorne is the teacher of a 'wise passiveness.' But to make clear his ideas of the supreme play of Providence in human affairs, he needs in some sort to reduce the reverence for individuality by a strange mixing and conglomeration of motives. The good are not wholly good with him; neither are the worst of men wholly bad. The very goodness of the best, however, when it is reckoned on as goodness, may become an evil, and the shame of the sinner may be translated into a source of blessedness by the ministry of atonement. Hester Prynne's scarlet letter transforms itself into a painful bliss in her little Pearl ; but Arthur Dimmesdale's scarlet letter, hidden from the eyes of all, burns into his very heart. And so, because of the casuistical constructions and the necessary apologies for some forms of transgression, Hawthorne does tend to somewhat confuse settled conventional moral judgments. But he could only do this with the thoughtless or the ill-disciplined. There never is the shade of oblique reference to true nobleness, or to real devotion, however opposed the object of it may be to what he himself would elect. Nothing could be finer than his sympathy at once for Endicott and the gay young Lord and Lady of the May, in his story of ' The Maypole of Merry Mount.'

His morality is of the noblest. It is the consecration of unselfishness. All things yield to self-sacrifice. This is the perpetual miracle-worker. With what skill he shows us how Phœbe Pyncheon yields up her very life for Clifford and Hepzibah. Poor Phœbe ! It seemed that she was giving up her sunshine, her youth and all its heritage, for them

She half-ruefully says : ' Ah, me ! I shall never be so merry as before I knew Cousin Hepzibah and poor Cousin Clifford. I have grown a great deal older in this little time. *I have given them my sunshine, and have been glad to give it ; but, of course, I cannot both give and keep it. They are welcome notwithstanding.*' And yet Holgrave replies : ' *You have lost nothing, Phœbe, worth keeping, nor which it was possible to keep.* Our first faith is of no value ; for we are never conscious of it till after it has gone. I shouldn't wonder if Clifford were to crumble away some morning after you are gone, and nothing be seen of him more except a heap of dust. Miss Hepzibah, at any rate, will lose what little flexibility she has. They both exist by you.'

This is a cardinal idea in Hawthorne's theory of life. It often recurs. Giving up is truest gaining. That which robs us of what we most cherish is that which may most enrich. Our one business in life is to declare boldly for the soul. And if Hawthorne sometimes seemed unconsciously to do violence to cherished standards, he was, up to his measure, true to the deepest spirit of Christian teaching. A little note we have met with in one of our investigations leads us to conclude that this was to be the burden of the *Dolliver Romance*—that strange conception which was working itself into clearness in the mind of the Puritan poet when he was half consciously descending into the dark valley of the shadow :—

'I can't tell you,' he writes to the publisher, 'when to expect an instalment of the romance, if ever. There is something preternatural in my reluctance to begin. I linger at the threshold, and have a perception of very disagreeable phantasms to be encountered if I enter. I wish God had given me the faculty to write a sunshiny book. . . . *I want to prefix a little sketch of Thoreau to it, because, from a tradition which he told me about this house of mine, I got the idea of a deathless man, which is now taking a shape very different from the original one.* It seems the duty of a live literary man to perpetuate the memory of a dead one, when there is such fair opportunity as in this case ; but how Thoreau would scorn me for thinking that I could perpetuate him ! And I don't think so.'

'The idea of a deathless man !' And so old Dr. Dolliver, with his faculties all decayed, and his frail body almost visibly lapsing away, was to live on and on by virtue of his love for Panzie, to guard and watch over her, till he should be esteemed as deathless; and Panzie, like Phœbe Pyncheon, was joyously to give up her youth for his sake to prevent his shrunken body from falling into a heap of dust. She was to give him her sunshine, life, and youth; he was to give her wisdom, and hope, and by his love to dower her with the tranquil joy of that lovely purity of age, which is so quiet and reposeful in contrast with the hard bold purity of youth. The situation is one quite to Hawthorne's heart; and, though it seems not a likely one to be made powerfully interesting, he would have made it fascinating with touches of most quaint revelation.

We are debtors and creditors to each other, and our accounts can never be exactly balanced. The mysteries of life with Hawthorne close and centre here. He will not hear of perfect people. To be perfect were to be isolated. Those who are accredited with the possession of uncommon goodness, he is very apt to regard with suspicion. He loves unconscious goodness, and, like a certain shrewd poetess of our time, glories in childish naughtiness, if so be it is only *childlike*. The following shows him as the ruthless prober of ideals :—

' There being a discussion about Lord Byron on

the other side of the table, Mrs. N. spoke to me about Lady Byron, whom she knows intimately, characterising her as a most excellent and exemplary person, high-principled, unselfish, and now devoting herself to the care of her two grandchildren,—their mother, Byron's daughter, being dead. Lady Byron, she says, writes beautiful verses. *Somehow or other, all this praise, and more of the same kind, gave me an idea of an intolerably irreproachable person* ; and I asked Mrs. N. if Lady Byron were warm-hearted. With some hesitation, or mental reservation, at all events, not quite outspoken,—she answered that she was.'

As here, so in his fiction, Hawthorne is never for a moment lost in his own illusions. He looks coldly on the most beautiful shapes which he can conjure up before his imagination. He ruthlessly pricks his ideal to show how weak it is : and then calmly dips his pen in the blood to write out its story further, with a pale brightness of colouring, and a suggestion of higher perfection arising out of what appeared to be the fatal point of defect. His flowers nearly all grow out of graves. His sunshine is oppressive till it touches and is toned on shadow. Humanity is a mass of sores and blotches ; were it not for these, indeed, men would stagnate into stupidity and animalism. The world improves by dint of its errors ; for exceptional individual attainment is but the issue of disease. He is the Puritan casuist, preaching another kind of fatalism, in which the accepted ideals of life are not destroyed, but inverted. 'We go all wrong by a too strenuous resolution to go right ;' he urges, over and over again, which is an indirect accusation of want of faith, for which less cold observers than Hawthorne have often blamed the present age. Of all writers, however, it may be said that Hawthorne is the least dogmatic ; and of all books his tales are, perhaps, the least calculated to encourage positive ideas about human nature and human life. Rather it seems as though he was continually edging us on to paradoxes, that like shifting sands suck the shoes off our feet as we hasten onward, and all the more if they were weighted with defences to shield us from every chafe and injury. Shoes are good, but if the feet are being so crushed by them that we cannot walk barefooted, 'tis well that we should throw them aside so as to gain the free use of our feet even at the cost of some momentary suffering. Delusions can never be real and positive helps.

Much of Hawthorne's finest humour springs

from the fear lest he should be taken for a sentimentalist, and this, notwithstanding that he had
some of the symptoms of the sentimental disease.
He shrunk from publicity, and yet he sought it ;
confessing, with something of maladroitness as it
seems to us, in his preface to the 'Twice-Told Tales,'
that they were written to open a point of contact
with the world, and not for his own pleasure :
while yet, in the very same breath, the verdict of
the world is spoken of as having been but of little
moment to him, and is of little moment even now.
He sometimes unnecessarily depreciates himself
and his works out of concern lest he should seem
self-conscious. He is too strictly and stiffly on his
guard, taking rather too much 'care not to say
anything which the critics and the public may hear
that it is desirable to conceal.' As was said by a
person of good natural judgment, but of limited
literary culture, to whom we had given one of
Hawthorne's earlier stories to read, 'It is as if he
threw in some humour, in case he should seem to
be vain of his art.' And this is true. He has
little of the ordinary weakness of literary men in
the need for sympathy. In a vein of remarkable
self-assertion and self-depreciation, he would write
to his more intimate friends about his books.

This, for example, is part of a letter to Mr. Fields about 'Our Old Home':—

'Heaven sees fit to visit me with an unshakable conviction, that all this series of articles is good for nothing ; but that is none of my business, provided the public and you are of a different opinion. If you think any part of it can be left out with advantage, you are quite at liberty to do so. Probably I have not put Leigh Hunt quite high enough for your sentiments respecting him ; but no more genuine characterisation and criticism (so far as the writer's purpose to be true goes) was ever done. It is very slight. I might have made more of it but should not have improved it.'

He decries his own heroism, too, with a touch of cynical humour, even while heroically standing up for his friend. This is very significant; he is speaking of his determination to dedicate a book to Pierce, notwithstanding that the General had lost public favour, and was in a sense then pro- scribed :—

'I have no fancy for making myself a martyr when it is honourably and conscientiously possible to avoid it, *and I always measure out my heroism very accurately according to the exigencies of the occasion, and should be the last man in the world to throw a bit away needlessly.* So I have looked over the concluding paragraph, and have amended it in such a way that, while doing justice to my friend, it contains not a word that ought to be objectionable to any set of readers. If the public of the North see fit to ostracise me for this, I can only say that I would gladly sacrifice a thousand or two dollars rather than retain the goodwill of such a herd of dolts and mean-spirited scoundrels.'

His works are not stories at all in the sense we mean when we call Scott's novels stories. They are great allegories, in which human tendencies are artistically exhibited to us. Two of those now presented, 'Mother Rigby's Pipe,' and 'Passages from a Relinquished Work,' are very characteristic of him. Were one to judge merely from first impressions, one might very easily be misled as to the chief source of the fascination of Hawthorne's stories, which really lies in the subtle but almost imperceptible way in which real circumstances are constantly slipped into a medium the most shadowy and fantastic. The framework of real circumstances which he gives to ' The Scarlet Letter,' to ' Blithedale,' and to ' The Mosses from an Old Manse,' are only somewhat extreme illustrations of the way in which he everywhere sought to bring into intimate

contact the most shadowy and the most substantial elements in human nature.   His works
are thus the truest emblems of his life.   Brooding,
contemplative beyond most men, haunted by ideas
which seemed to demand for their complete
development a mind abstracted from the haze of
ordinary sympathies, he yet never abandoned himself to the joys of solitude, which at first soften and
expand, and then speedily cramp and freeze up the
finer feelings and benevolences.   He constantly
felt that his one chance of escape from the danger
peculiar to such dispositions as his, lay in more or
less real association with persons whose tastes and
ways of life were different from his own.   He himself, as we have seen, deliberately put on record his
opinion that nothing could be more beneficial for a
literary man than to be thrown among people who
did not sympathise with his pursuits, and whose
pursuits he had to go out of himself to appreciate.
To this peculiar feeling—for it was clearly something deeper than a conviction come at by any
process of reasoning—we may no doubt attribute
in great measure the steady patience and goodwill
with which he applied himself to the mechanical
duties he was called on to perform in the several
offices he held—the coal-weighing at Boston, and

the consular examinations at Liverpool. His stolid patience and good humour are indeed very remarkable in a man of such peculiar genius—a genius that led him by preference to take up the most morbid studies and abnormal conditions of life, and to make them the materials for romances. But, after all, this pertains to the very character of the man.   He seems imaginative, fanciful, working in materials that he may mould as fantastically as he pleases.   It is really the reverse.   He needs to gather his facts by a slow process of selection, consequent on the most inquisitorial investigation. He takes nothing on hearsay, but must test everything for himself.   As some physicians have found it needful to resort to experiments on themselves, the more surely to detect the virtues of certain subtle poisons, so Hawthorne must reduce all that is abnormal, morbid, and mixed in emotional experience into his own life.   And he absolutely needs the aid of facts as talismans wherewith to lure and master his own nature, and bend it the better to his purpose.   Old criminal trials, newspaper reports, even old advertisements, were a great treat to him.   He sometimes found mental aliment in the driest records ; and his intimate friends not seldom were surprised at his enthusiasm over such things. One of them tells how, having heard him speak of his love for such writings, he picked up one day a set of old English State-Trials and sent them to Hawthorne, who declared that he spent more hours over them and got more delectation out of them than tongue could tell. If five lives were vouchsafed to him, he said, that he could employ them all in writing stories from these books. He had sketched in his mind various romances founded on the remarkable trials there reported, and one day he made the said friend's blood tingle by relating to him some of the situations which he intended to weave into these romances. In one place he says that 'The Diary of a Coroner' would be a fine subject. There can be no doubt that there was a certain vein of realism in him which would have enabled him to treat such a theme in a wonderfully effective way. No doubt it was this conviction which made one of his French translators rank 'The Journal of an African Cruiser' as an original work of imagination. He writes :—'Outre les œuvrages que nous venons de citer, on a de lui " L'Image de Neige et autres Contes," le " Journal d'une Croisière en Afrique " (!), le " Livre des Merveilles," le " Fauteuil du Grand-papa," et " Les Contes de Tanglewood.' "

It is on account of their letting us, far more completely than could have been done otherwise, into the secret processes of his art, that his note-books are, from a critical point of view, so inexpressibly valuable. Where they are least interesting in themselves, they are all the richer in this regard. They show us how closely this great man studied his themes; how conscientious, how careful he was not to commit himself in any way; how persistently he returned to his work again and again; and how difficult he found it to bring anything up to the high level of his own exacting judgment. Every page, free, sparkling, graceful as it seems, is the result of long, unwearied labour and meditation. He wrought on the same principle as any anatomist, taking nothing for granted. If he hears of a murder of specially horrible character, where the motives that led to it are so mixed and involved as to force from us the admission that, after all, a thread of something not wholly dark and diabolic runs through the perpetrator's thoughts and feelings, he must first microscopically examine every fact and detail with the watchful brain of a detective, so that he may be able to place himself in the very position of the criminal, and faithfully report on his mood, and all the varying influences that led to it. After the publication of 'The Scarlet Letter,' we read that he was constantly applied to by criminals and others for advice and help.

Hawthorne was in many ways a 'confessor;' and in his most repulsive subjects and characters there is a slight air as of justification for the wrongdoer. A kind of subdued apology for the vileness of human nature runs through his writings. This is not because he held light views as to duty—his views of duty were as strict and as high as those of any of his Puritan ancestors ; but, as has been said, he desires to see everything in relation to a prevailing Providence ; and the necessity that lies on him, in order to make this the better apparent, to rigidly reduce the claims of individuals, leads him almost of set purpose to mix and conglomerate motives. He himself has written, 'Blessed are all simple emotions be they bright or dark; it is only the mixture of them that is infernal.' But in spite of this he dealt in mixed emotions till it would almost seem as though he had no taste for simpler ones, or had wholly lost the faculty of interesting himself in them ; as those who have been accustomed to highly spiced food and drink, cannot bring themselves afterwards to relish foods and drinks that are pure and unmixed. It was his morality and his need for actual contact with men, that saved him from the last and worst results of cynicism. He is no hero-worshipper. He sees too clearly into human nature, and detects its seamy places far too easily to be a sentimentalist in any form. But he is in the best sense a believer, though not perhaps after the precise orthodox type. He has the firmest faith in a divine purpose that embraces all man's puny efforts, and takes them up and includes them, to educe from them at last a largesse of benefit for humanity, however far the individuals themselves may have failed to recognise, or to reach up to the height of, this divine design. And thus, notwithstanding that he is sometimes very divided as to several open courses of human action, he never really doubts. The more we get to know him we feel the more surely that he is a genuine believer in goodness and in God. In spite of his strange curiosity, which cannot even be restrained in face of the most perilous problems, he still keeps intact a region of his spiritual nature sacred to mystery. This man, with his 'awful in-sight,' and his morbid melancholy, yet held firmly by the spiritual world, refusing to surrender the inmost citadel. Here he takes his position with the most commonplace of men; and in this lies one element of his greatness. His works, while they may sometimes raise question as to conventional judgments on this or that action, always encourage the deepest reverence for the spirit of man itself—from which flows unceasingly the true morality that ever renews itself in love and sympathy. And he always will, on this account, be most truly appreciated by close students of human nature; while the ghostliness of his imagination gives him sometimes a strange fascination, which all alike must feel, and recognise the strength that lay behind it.

Of his qualities as a writer what need is there to speak? No man has ever used the English language with more perfect grace and self-control than he has done, no man has more skilfully brought out its more secret chords and harmonies. His words fit his thoughts, as neatly as do the coverings which nature provides for her finest and most delicate productions—chaste ornament never being spared.

I.

' DICKON,' cried Mother Rigby, 'a coal for my pipe!'

The pipe was in the old dame's mouth when she said these words. She had thrust it there after filling it with tobacco, but without stooping to light it at the hearth, where indeed there was no appearance of a fire having been kindled that morning. Forthwith, however, as soon as the order was given, there was an intense red glow out of the bowl of the pipe, and a whiff of smoke from Mother Rigby's lips. Whence the coal came, and how brought thither by an invisible hand, I have never been able to discover.

'Good!' quoth Mother Rigby, with a nod

of her head, 'thank ye, Dickon! And now for making this scarecrow. Be within call, Dickon, in case I need you again.'

The good woman had risen thus early, (for as yet it was scarcely sunrise,) in order to set about making a scarecrow, which she intended to put in the middle of her corn-patch. It was now the latter week of May, and the crows and blackbirds had already discovered the little, green, rolled-up leaf of the Indian corn just peeping out of the soil. She was determined, therefore, to contrive as lifelike a scarecrow as ever was seen, and finish it immediately, from top to toe, so that it should begin its sentinel's duty that very morning. Now Mother Rigby, (as everybody must have heard,) was one of the most cunning and potent witches in New England, and might, with very little trouble, have made a scarecrow ugly enough to frighten the minister himself. But on this occasion, as she had awakened in an uncommonly pleasant humour, and was further dulcified by her pipe of tobacco, she resolved to produce something fine, beautiful, and splendid, rather than hideous and horrible.

'I don't want to set up a hobgoblin in my own corn-patch, and almost at my own door-step,' said Mother Rigby to herself, puffing out a whiff of smoke: 'I could do it if I pleased, but I'm tired of doing marvellous things, and so I'll keep within the bounds of everyday business, just for variety's sake. Besides, there is no use in scaring the little children for a mild roundabout, though 'tis true I'm a witch.'

It was settled, therefore, in her own mind, that the scarecrow should represent a fine gentleman of the period, so far as the materials at hand would allow. Perhaps it may be as well to enumerate the chief of the articles that went to the composition of this figure.

The most important item of all, probably, although it made so little show, was a certain broomstick, on which Mother Rigby had taken many an airy gallop at midnight, and which now served the scarecrow by way of a

spinal column, or, as the unlearned phrase it,
a backbone. One of its arms was a disabled
flail which used to be wielded by Goodman
Rigby, before his spouse worried him out of
this troublesome world ; the other, if I mistake not, was composed of the pudding stick
and a broken rung of a chair, tied loosely
together at the elbow. As for its legs, the
right was a hoe handle, and the left an undis-
tinguished and miscellaneous stick from the
woodpile.   Its lungs, stomach, and other
affairs of that kind were nothing better than
a meal bag stuffed with straw. Thus we
have made out the skeleton and entire corpo-
ricity of the scarecrow, with the exception of
his head ; and this was admirably supplied
by a somewhat withered and shrivelled pumpkin, in which Mother Rigby cut two holes
for the eyes, and a slit for the mouth, leaving
a bluish-coloured knob in the middle to pass
for a nose.   It was really quite a respectable
face.

   ' I've seen worse ones on human shoulders,
at any rate,' said Mother Rigby.   ' And

many a fine gentleman has a pumpkin head, as well as my scarecrow.'

But the clothes, in this case, were to be the making of the man. So the good old woman took down from a peg an ancient plum-coloured coat of London make, and with relics of embroidery on its seams, cuffs, pocket-flaps, and button-holes, but lamentably worn and faded, patched at the elbows, tattered at the skirts, and threadbare all over. On the left breast was a round hole, whence either a star of nobility had been rent away, or else the hot heart of some former wearer had scorched it through and through. The neighbours said that this rich garment belonged to the Black Man's wardrobe, and that he kept it at Mother Rigby's cottage for the convenience of slipping it on whenever he wished to make a grand appearance at the governor's table. To match the coat there was a velvet waistcoat of very ample size and formerly embroidered with foliage that had been as brightly golden as the maple leaves in October, but which had now quite vanished out of the substance of the velvet. Next came a pair of scarlet breeches, once worn by the French governor of Louisbourg, and the knees of which had touched the lower step of the throne of Louis le Grand. The Frenchman had given these smallclothes to an Indian powwow, who parted with them to the old witch for a gill of strong waters, at one of their dances in the forest. Furthermore, Mother Rigby produced a pair of silk stockings and put them on the figure's legs, where they showed as unsubstantial as a dream, with the wooden reality of the sticks making itself miserably apparent through the holes. Lastly, she put her dead husband's wig on the bare scalp of the pumpkin, and surmounted the whole with a dusty three-cornered hat, in which was stuck the longest tail feather of a rooster.

Then the old dame stood the figure up in a corner of her cottage, and chuckled to behold its yellow semblance of a visage, with its nobby little nose thrust into the air. It had a strangely self-satisfied aspect, and seemed to say, 'Come, look at me!'

'And you are well worth looking at, that's a fact!' quoth Mother Rigby, in admiration of her own handiwork! 'I've made many a puppet since I've been a witch; but methinks this is the finest of them all. 'Tis almost too good for a scarecrow. And, by the by, I'll just fill a fresh pipe of tobacco, and then take him out to the corn-patch.'

While filling her pipe, the old woman continued to gaze with almost motherly affection at the figure in the corner. To say the truth, whether it were chance, or skill, or downright witchcraft, there was something wonderfully human in this ridiculous shape, bedizened with its tattered finery; and as for the countenance, it appeared to shrivel its yellow surface into a grin—a funny kind of expression betwixt scorn and merriment, as if it understood itself to be a jest at mankind. The more Mother Rigby looked, the better she was pleased.

'Dickon,' cried she sharply, 'another coal for my pipe!'

Hardly had she spoken, when, just as

before, there was a red-glowing coal on the top of the tobacco. She drew in a long whiff and puffed it forth again into the bar of morning sunshine which struggled through the one dusty pane of her cottage window. Mother Rigby always liked to flavour her pipe with a coal of fire from the particular chimney corner whence this had been brought. But where that chimney corner might be, or who brought the coal from it—further than that the invisible messenger seemed to respond to the name of Dickon—I cannot tell.

'That puppet yonder,' thought Mother Rigby, still with her eyes fixed on the scarecrow, 'is too good a piece of work to stand all summer in a corn-patch, frightening away the crows and blackbirds. He's capable of better things. Why, I've danced with a worse one, when partners happened to be scarce, at our witch meetings in the forest! What if I should let him take his chance among other men of straw and empty fellows who go bustling about the world?'

The old witch took three or four more whiffs of her pipe and smiled.

'He'll meet plenty of his brethren at every street-corner!' continued she. 'Well; I didn't mean to dabble in witchcraft to-day, further than the lighting of my pipe; but a witch I am, and a witch I'm likely to be, and there's no use trying to shirk it. I'll make a man of my scarecrow, were it only for the joke's sake!'

While muttering these words, Mother Rigby took the pipe from her own mouth and thrust it into the crevice which represented the same feature in the pumpkin visage of the scarecrow.

'Puff, darling, puff!' said she. 'Puff away, my fine fellow! your life depends upon it!'

This was a strange exhortation, undoubtedly, to be addressed to a mere thing of sticks, straw, and old clothes, with nothing better than a shrivelled pumpkin for a head; as we know to have been the scarecrow's case. Nevertheless, as we must carefully hold in remembrance, Mother Rigby was a witch of singular power and dexterity; and, keeping this fact duly before our minds, we shall see nothing beyond credibility in the remarkable incidents of our story. Indeed, the great difficulty will be at once got over, if we can only bring ourselves to believe that, as soon as the old dame bade him puff, there came a whiff of smoke from the scarecrow's mouth. It was the very feeblest of whiffs, to be sure; but it was followed by another and another, each more decided than the preceding one.

'Puff away, my pet! puff away, my pretty one!' Mother Rigby kept repeating, with her pleasantest smile. 'It is the breath of life to ye; and that you may take my word for.'

Beyond all question the pipe was bewitched. There must have been a spell either in the tobacco, or in the fiercely-glowing coal that so mysteriously burned on the top of it, or in the pungently aromatic smoke which exhaled from the kindled weed. The figure, after a few doubtful attempts, at length blew forth a volley of smoke extending all the way from the obscure corner into the bar of sunshine. There it eddied and melted away among the motes of dust. It seemed a convulsive effort; for the two or three next whiffs were fainter, although the coal still glowed and threw a gleam over the scarecrow's visage. The old witch clapped her skinny hands together, and smiled encouragingly upon her handiwork. She saw that the charm worked well. The shrivelled, yellow face, which heretofore had been no face at all, had already a thin, fantastic haze, as it were, of human likeness, shifting to and fro across it; sometimes vanishing entirely, but growing more perceptible than ever with the next whiff from the pipe. The whole figure, in like manner, assumed a show of life, such as we impart to ill-defined shapes among the clouds, and half deceive ourselves with the pastime of our own fancy.

If we must needs pry closely into the matter, it may be doubted whether there was any real change, after all, in the sordid, worn-out, worthless, and ill-jointed substance of the scare-crow; but merely a spectral illusion, and a cunning effect of light and shade so coloured and contrived as to delude the eyes of most men. The miracles of witchcraft seem always to have had a very shallow subtlety; and, at least, if the above explanation do not hit the truth of the process, I can suggest no better.

'Well puffed, my pretty lad!' still cried old Mother Rigby. 'Come, another good stout whiff, and let it be with might and main. Puff for thy life, I tell thee! Puff out of the very bottom of thy heart; if any heart thou hast, or any bottom to it! Well done, again! Thou did'st suck in that mouthful as if for the pure love of it.'

And then the witch beckoned to the scarecrow, throwing so much magnetic po-tency into her gesture that it seemed as if it must inevitably be obeyed, like the mystic call of the loadstone when it summons the iron.

'Why lurkest thou in the corner, lazy one?'

said she. 'Step forth! Thou hast the world before thee!'

Upon my word, if the legend were not one which I heard on my grandmother's knee, and which had established its place among things credible before my childish judgment could analyse its probability, I question whether I should have the face to tell it now.

In obedience to Mother Rigby's word, and extending its arm as if to reach her outstretched hand, the figure made a step forward—a kind of hitch and jerk, however, rather than a step —then tottered and almost lost its balance. What could the witch expect? It was nothing, after all, but a scarecrow stuck upon two sticks. But the strong-willed old beldam scowled, and beckoned, and flung the energy of her purpose so forcibly at this poor combination of rotten wood, and musty straw, and ragged garments, that it was compelled to show itself a man, in spite of the reality of things. So it stepped into the bar of sunshine. There it stood— poor devil of a contrivance that it was!— with only the thinnest vesture of human similitude about it, through which was evident the stiff, ricketty, incongruous, faded, tattered, good-for-nothing patchwork of its substance, ready to sink in a heap upon the floor, as conscious of its own unworthiness to be erect. Shall I confess the truth? At its present point of vivification, the scarecrow reminds me of some of the lukewarm and abortive characters, composed of heterogeneous materials, used for the thousandth time, and never worth using, with which romance writers, (and myself, no doubt, among the rest,) have so over-peopled the world of fiction.

But the fierce old hag began to get angry and show a glimpse of her diabolic nature, (like a snake's head, peeping with a hiss out of her bosom,) at this pusillanimous behaviour of the thing which she had taken the trouble to put together.

'Puff away, wretch!' cried she wrathfully. Puff, puff, puff, thou thing of straw and emptiness! thou rag or two! thou meal bag! thou pumpkin head! thou nothing! Where shall I find a name vile enough to call thee by? Puff, I say, and suck in thy fantastic life along with the smoke; else I snatch the pipe from thy mouth and hurl thee where that red coal came from.'

Thus threatened, the unhappy scarecrow had nothing for it but to puff away for dear life. As need was, therefore, it applied itself lustily to the pipe, and sent forth such abundant volleys of tobacco smoke that the small cottage became all vaporous. The one sunbeam struggled mistily through, and could but imperfectly define the image of the cracked and dusty window pane on the opposite wall. Mother Rigby, meanwhile, with one brown arm akimbo and the other stretched towards the figure, loomed grimly amid the obscurity with such port and expression as when she was wont to heave a ponderous nightmare on her victims, and stand at the bedside to enjoy their agony. In fear and trembling did this poor scarecrow puff. But its efforts, it must be acknowledged, served an excellent purpose; for, with each successive whiff, the figure lost more and more of its dizzy and perplexing tenuity and seemed to take denser substance. Its very garments, moreover, partook of the magical change, and shone with the gloss of novelty and glistened with the skilfully embroidered gold that had long been rent away. And, half-revealed among the smoke, a yellow visage bent its lustreless eyes on Mother Rigby.

At last the old witch clinched her fist and shook it at the figure. Not that she was positively angry, but merely acting on the principle—perhaps untrue, or not the only truth, though as high a one as Mother Rigby could be expected to attain—that feeble and torpid natures, being incapable of better inspiration, must be stirred up by fear. But here was the crisis. Should she fail in what she now sought to effect, it was her ruthless purpose to scatter the miserable simulacre into its original elements.

'Thou hast a man's aspect,' said she, sternly. 'Have also the echo and mockery of a voice! I bid thee speak!'

The scarecrow gasped, struggled, and at
length emitted a murmur, which was so incorporated with its smoky breath that you
could scarcely tell whether it were indeed a
voice or only a whiff of tobacco. Some
narrators of this legend hold the opinion that
Mother Rigby's conjurations and the fierceness of her will had compelled a familiar
spirit into the figure, and that the voice was
his.

'Mother,' mumbled the poor stifled voice,
' be not so awful with me ! I would fain speak ;
but being without wits, what can I say ?'

'Thou canst speak, darling, canst thou ?'
cried Mother Rigby, relaxing her grim countenance into a smile. 'And what shalt
thou say, quotha! Say, indeed! Art thou of
the brotherhood of the empty skull, and de-
mandest of me what thou shalt say ? Thou
shalt say a thousand things, and saying them
a thousand times over, thou shalt still have
said nothing ! Be not afraid, I tell thee!
When thou comest into the world, (whither I
purpose sending thee forthwith,) thou shalt

not lack the wherewithal to talk. Talk! Why thou shalt babble like a mill-stream, if thou wilt. Thou hast brains enough for that, I trow!'

'At your service, mother,' responded the figure.

'And that was well said, my pretty one,' answered Mother Rigby. 'Then thou spakest like thyself, and meant nothing. Thou shalt have a hundred such set phrases, and five hundred to the boot of them. And now, darling, I have taken so much pains with thee, and thou art so beautiful, that, by my troth, I love thee better than any witch's puppet in the world; and I've made them of all sorts—clay, wax, straw, sticks, night-fog, morning-mist, sea-foam, and chimney-smoke. But thou art the very best. So give heed to what I say.'

'Yes, kind mother,' said the figure, 'with all my heart!'

'With all thy heart!' cried the old witch, setting her hands to her sides and laughing loudly. 'Thou hast such a pretty way of speaking. With all thy heart! And thou didst put thy hand to the left side of thy waistcoat as if thou really hadst one!'

So now, in high good humour with this fantastic contrivance of hers, Mother Rigby told the scarecrow that it must go and play its part in the great world, where not one man in a hundred, she affirmed, was gifted with more real substance than itself. And, that he might hold up his head with the best of them, she endowed him, on the spot, with an unreckonable amount of wealth. It consisted partly of a gold mine in Eldorado, and of ten thousand shares in a broken bubble, and of half a million of acres of vineyard at the North Pole, and of a castle in the air, and a château in Spain, together with all the rents and income therefrom accruing. She further made over to him the cargo of a certain ship, laden with salt from Cadiz, which she herself, by her necromantic arts, had caused to founder, ten years before, in the deepest part of mid-ocean. If the salt were not dissolved, and could be brought to market, it would fetch a pretty penny among the fishermen. That she might not lack ready money, she gave him a copper farthing of Birmingham manufacture, being all the coin she had about her, and likewise a great deal of brass, which she applied to his forehead, thus making it yellower than ever.

'With that brass alone,' quoth Mother Rigby,' thou canst pay thy way over all the earth. Kiss me, pretty darling! I have done my best for thee.'

Furthermore, that the adventurer might lack no possible advantage towards a fair start in life, this excellent old dame gave him a token by which he was to introduce himself to a certain magistrate, member of the council, merchant, and elder of the Church, (the four capacities constituting but one man,) who stood at the head of society in the neighbouring metropolis. The token was neither more nor less than a single word, which Mother Rigby whispered to the scarecrow, and which the scarecrow was to whisper to the merchant.

'Gouty as the old fellow is, he'll run thy

errands for thee, when once thou hast given him that word in his ear,' said the old witch. ' Mother Rigby knows the worshipful Justice Gookin, and the worshipful Justice knows Mother Rigby!'

Here the witch thrust her wrinkled face close to the puppet's, chuckling irrepressibly, and fidgetting all through her system with delight at the idea which she meant to communicate.

' The worshipful Master Gookin,' whispered she, "hath a comely maiden to his daughter. And hark ye, my pet! Thou hast a fair outside, and a pretty wit enough of thine own. Yea, a pretty wit enough! Thou wilt think better of it when thou hast seen more of other people's wits. Now, with thy outside and thy inside, thou art the very man to win a young girl's heart. Never doubt it! I tell thee it shall be so. Put but a bold face on the matter; sigh, smile, flourish thy hat, thrust forth thy leg like a dancing master, put thy right hand to the left side of thy waistcoat, and pretty Polly Gookin is thine own!'

All this while the new creature had been sucking in and exhaling the vapoury fragrance of his pipe, and seemed now to continue this occupation as much for the enjoyment it afforded as because it was an essential condition of his existence. It was wonderful to see how exceedingly like a human being it behaved. Its eyes, (for it appeared to possess a pair,) were bent on Mother Rigby, and at suitable junctures it nodded or shook its head. Neither did it lack words suitable for the occasion: 'Really! Indeed! Pray tell me! Is it possible! Upon my word! By no means! O! Ah! Hem!' and other such weighty utterances as imply attention, inquiry, acquiescence, or dissent· on the part of the auditor. Even had you stood by and seen the scarecrow made, you could scarcely have resisted the conviction that it perfectly understood the cunning counsels which the old witch poured into its counterfeit of an ear. The more earnestly it applied its lips to the pipe the more distinctly was its human likeness stamped among visible realities, the more sagacious grew its expression, the more lifelike its gestures and movements, and the more intelligibly audible its voice. Its garments, too, glistened so much the brighter with an illusory magnificence. The very pipe, in which burned the spell of all this wonder-work, ceased to appear as a smoke-blackened earthen-stump, and became a meerschaum, with painted bowl and amber mouth-piece.

It might be apprehended, however, that as the life of the illusion seemed identical with the vapour of the pipe, it would terminate simultaneously with the reduction of the tobacco to ashes. But the beldam foresaw the difficulty.

'Hold thou the pipe, my precious one,' said she, 'while I fill it for thee again.'

It was sorrowful to behold how the fine gentleman began to fade back into a scarecrow while Mother Rigby shook the ashes out of the pipe and proceeded to replenish it from her tobacco-box.

'Dickon,' cried she, in her high, sharp tone, 'another coal for this pipe!'

No sooner said than the intensely red speck of fire was glowing within the pipe-bowl; and the scarecrow, without waiting for the witch's bidding, applied the tube to his lips and drew in a few short, convulsive whiffs, which soon, however, became regular and equable.

'Now, mine own heart's darling,' quoth Mother Rigby, 'whatever may happen to thee, thou must stick to thy pipe. Thy life is in it; and that, at least, thou knowest well, if thou knowest nought besides. Stick to thy pipe, I say! Smoke, puff, blow thy cloud; and tell the people, if any question be made, that it is for thy health, and that so the physician orders thee to do. And, sweet one, when thou shalt find thy pipe getting low, go apart into some corner, and, (first filling thyself with smoke,) cry sharply, "Dickon, a fresh pipe of tobacco! and, Dickon, another coal for my pipe!" and have it into thy pretty mouth as speedily as may be. Else, instead of a gallant gentleman in a gold-laced coat, thou wilt be but a jumble of sticks and tattered clothes, and a bag of straw, and a withered pumpkin! Now depart, my treasure, and good luck go with thee!'

'Never fear, mother!' said the figure, in a stout voice, and sending forth a courageous whiff of smoke, 'I will thrive, if an honest man and a gentleman may!'

'O thou wilt be the death of me!' cried the old witch, convulsed with laughter. 'That was well said. If an honest man and a gentleman may! Thou playest thy part to perfection. Get along with thee for a smart fellow; and I will wager on thy head, as a man of pith and substance, with a brain, and what they call a heart, and all else that a man should have, against any other thing on two legs. I hold myself a better witch than yesterday, for thy sake. Did not I make thee? And I defy any witch in New England to make such another! Here; take thy staff along with thee!'

The staff, though it was but a plain oaken stick, immediately took the aspect of a gold-headed cane.

' That gold head has as much sense in it as thine own,' said Mother Rigby, 'and it will guide thee straight to worshipful Master Gookin's door. Get thee gone, my pretty pet, my darling, my precious one, my treasure ; and if anyone ask thy name, it is Feathertop. For thou hast a feather in thy hat, and I have thrust a handful of feathers into the hollow of thy head, and thy wig, too, is of the fashion they call Feathertop,—so be Feathertop thy name !'

And, issuing from the cottage, Feathertop strode manfully towards town. Mother Rigby stood at the threshold, well-pleased to see how the sunbeams glistened on him, as if all his magnificence were real, and how diligently and lovingly he smoked his pipe, and how handsomely he walked, in spite of a little stiffness of his legs. She watched him until out of sight, and threw a witch benediction after her darling, when a turn of the road snatched him from her view.

II.

BETIMES in the forenoon, when the principal street of the neighbouring town was just at its acme of life and bustle, a stranger of very distinguished figure was seen on the side-walk. His port as well as his garments betokened nothing short of nobility. He wore a richly-embroidered plum-coloured coat, a waistcoat of costly velvet magnificently adorned with golden foliage, a pair of splendid scarlet breeches, and the finest and glossiest of white silk stockings. His head was covered with a peruke, so daintily powdered and adjusted that it would have been sacrilege to disorder it with a hat; which, therefore, (and it was a gold-laced hat, set off with a snowy feather,) he carried beneath his arm. On the breast of his coat glistened a star. He managed his gold-headed cane with an airy grace peculiar to the fine gentleman of the period ;

and, to give the highest possible finish to his equipment, he had lace ruffles at his wrist, of a most ethereal delicacy, sufficiently avouching how idle and aristocratic must be the hands which they half concealed.

It was a remarkable point in the accoutrement of this brilliant personage, that he held in his left hand a fantastic kind of a pipe, with an exquisitely painted bowl and an amber mouthpiece. This he applied to his lips as often as every five or six paces, and inhaled a deep whiff of smoke, which, after being retained a moment in his lungs, might be seen to eddy gracefully from his mouth and nostrils.

As may well be supposed, the street was all astir to find out the stranger's name.

'It is some great nobleman, beyond question,' said one of the townspeople. 'Do you see the star at his breast ?'

'Nay; it is too bright to be seen,' said another. 'Yes; he must needs be a nobleman as you say. But by what conveyance, think you, can his lordship have voyaged or travelled hither? There has been no vessel from the old country for a month past; and if he have arrived overland from the southward, pray where are his attendants and equipage?'

'He needs no equipage to set off his rank,' remarked a third. 'If he came among us in rags, nobility would shine through a hole in his elbow. I never saw such dignity of aspect. He has the old Norman blood in his veins, I warrant him.'

'I rather take him to be a Dutchman, or one of your high Germans,' said another citizen. 'The men of those countries have always the pipe at their mouths.'

'And so has a Turk,' answered his companion. 'But, in my judgment, this stranger hath been bred at the French court, and hath there learned politeness and grace of manner, which none understand so well as the nobility of France. What gait, now! A vulgar spectator might deem it stiff—he might call it a hitch and a jerk—but, to my eye, it hath an unspeakable majesty, and must have been acquired by constant observation of the deportment of the Grand Monarque. The stranger's character and office are evident enough. He is a French ambassador, come to treat with our rulers about the cession of Canada.'

'More probably a Spaniard,' said another, 'and hence his yellow complexion ; or, most likely, he is from the Havanas, or from some port on the Spanish main, and comes to make investigation about the piracies which our governor is thought to connive at. Those settlers in Peru and Mexico have skins as yellow as the gold which they dig out of their mines.'

'Yellow or not,' cried a lady, 'he is a beautiful man!—so tall, so slender! such a fine, noble face, with so well-shaped a nose, and all that delicacy of expression about the mouth. And, bless me, how bright his star is! It positively shoots out flames!'

'So do your eyes, fair lady,' said the stranger, with a bow and a flourish of his pipe; for he was just passing at the instant.

'Upon my honour, they have quite dazzled me.'

'Was ever so original and exquisite a compliment?' murmured the lady, in an ecstasy of delight.

Amid the general admiration excited by the stranger's appearance, there were only two dissentient voices. One was that of an impertinent cur, which, after snuffing at the heels of the glistening figure, put its tail between its legs and skulked into its master's back yard, vociferating an execrable howl. The other dissentient was a young child, who squalled at the fullest stretch of his lungs, and babbled some unintelligible nonsense about a pumpkin.

Feathertop meanwhile pursued his way along the street. Except for the few complimentary words to the lady, and now and then a slight inclination of the head in requital of the profound reverences of the bystanders, he seemed wholly absorbed in his pipe. There needed no other proof of his rank and consequence than the perfect equanimity with which he comported himself, while the curiosity and admiration of the town swelled into a clamour around him. With a crowd gathering behind his footsteps, he finally reached the mansion-house of the worshipful Justice Gookin, entered the gate, ascended the steps of the front door, and knocked. In the interim, before his summons was answered, the stranger was observed to shake the ashes out of his pipe.

'What did he say in that sharp voice?' inquired one of the spectators.

'Nay, I know not,' answered his friend. 'But the sun dazzles my eyes strangely. How dim and faded his lordship looks all of a sudden! Bless my wits, what is the matter with me?'

'The wonder is,' said the other, that his pipe, which was out only an instant ago, should be all alight again, and with the reddest coal I ever saw. There is something mysterious about this stranger. What a whiff of smoke was that! Dim and faded did you

call him ?   Why, as he turns about, the star
on his breast is all ablaze.'

'It is, indeed,' said his companion ; 'and
it will go near to dazzle pretty Polly
Gookin, whom I see peering at it out of the
chamber window.'

The door being now opened, Feathertop
turned to the crowd, made a stately bend of
his body like a great man acknowledging the
reverence of the meaner sort, and vanished
into the house. There was a mysterious kind
of a smile, if it might not better be called a
grin or grimace, upon his visage ; but, of all
the throng that beheld him, not an individual
appears to have possessed insight enough to
detect the illusive character of the stranger
except a little child and a cur dog.

Our legend here loses somewhat of its con-
tinuity, and, passing over the preliminary explanation between Feathertop and the merchant, goes in quest of the pretty Polly
Gookin. She was a damsel of a soft, round
figure, with light hair and blue eyes, and a
fair, rosy face, which seemed neither very

shrewd nor very simple. This young lady had caught a glimpse of the glistening stranger while standing at the threshold, and had forthwith put on a laced cap, a string of beads, her finest kerchief, and her stiffest damask petticoat, in preparation for the interview. Hurrying from her chamber to the parlour, she had ever since been viewing herself in the large looking-glass and practising pretty airs—now a smile, now a ceremonious dignity of aspect, and now a softer smile than the former, kissing her hand likewise, tossing her head, and managing her fan ; while within the mirror an unsubstantial little maid repeated every gesture, and did all the foolish things that Polly did, but without making her ashamed of them. In short, it was the fault of pretty Polly's ability rather than her will if she failed to be as complete an artifice as the illustrious Feathertop himself; and, when she thus tampered with her own simplicity, the witch's phantom might well hope to win her.

No sooner did Polly hear her father's gouty

footsteps approaching the parlour door, accompanied with the stiff clatter of Featherton's high-heeled shoes, than she seated herself bolt upright and innocently began warbling a song.

'Polly! daughter Polly!' cried the old merchant. 'Come hither, child.'

Master Gookin's aspect, as he opened the door, was doubtful and troubled.

'This gentleman,' continued he, presenting the stranger, 'is the Chevalier Feathertop,—nay, I beg his pardon, my Lord Feathertop,—who hath brought me a token of remembrance from an ancient friend of mine. Pay your duty to his lordship, child, and honour him as his quality deserves.'

After these few words of introduction the worshipful magistrate immediately quitted the room. But, even in that brief moment, had the fair Polly glanced aside at her father instead of devoting herself wholly to the brilliant guest, she might have taken warning of some mischief nigh at hand. The old man was nervous, fidgety and very pale. Purposing

a smile of courtesy, he had deformed his face
with a sort of galvanic grin, which, when
Feathertop's back was turned, he exchanged
for a scowl, at the same time shaking his fist
and stamping his gouty foot—an incivility
which brought its retribution along with it.
The truth appears to have been, that
Mother's Rigby's word of introduction, whatever it might be, had operated far more on the
rich merchant's fears than on his good-will.
Moreover, being a man of wonderfully acute
observation, he had noticed that the painted
figures on the bowl of Feathertop's pipe were
in motion. Looking more closely, he became
convinced that these figures were a party of
little demons, each duly provided with horns
and a tail, and dancing hand in hand, with
gestures of diabolical merriment, round the
circumference of the pipe bowl. As if to
confirm his suspicions, while Master Gookin
ushered his guest along a dusky passage from
his private room to the parlour, the star on
Feathertop's breast had scintillated actual

flames, and threw a flickering gleam upon the wall, the ceiling, and the floor.

With such sinister prognostics manifesting themselves on all hands, it is not to be marvelled at that the merchant should have felt that he was committing his daughter to a very questionable acquaintance. He cursed, in his secret soul, the insinuating elegance of Feathertop's manners, as this brilliant personage bowed, smiled, put his hand on his heart, inhaled a long whiff from his pipe, and enriched the atmosphere with the smoky vapour of a fragrant and visible sigh. Gladly would poor Master Gookin have thrust his dangerous guest into the street; but there was a constraint and terror within him. This respectable old gentlemen, we fear, at an earlier period of life, had given some pledge or other to the evil principle, and perhaps was now to redeem it by the sacrifice of his daughter.

It so happened that the parlour door was partly of glass, shaded by a silken curtain, the folds of which hung a little awry. So

strong was the merchant's interest in wit-
nessing what was to ensue between the fair
Polly and the gallant Feathertop that after
quitting the room he could by no means
refrain from peeping through the crevice of
the curtain.

But there was nothing very miraculous
to be seen ; nothing—except the trifles previously noticed—to confirm the idea of a
supernatural peril environing the pretty
Polly. The stranger, it is true, was evidently
a thorough and practised man of the world,
systematic and self-possessed, and therefore
the sort of a person to whom a parent ought
not to confide a simple, young girl without
due watchfulness for the result. The worthy
magistrate, who had been conversant with
all degrees and qualities of mankind, could
not but perceive every motion and gesture of
the distinguished Feathertop come in its
proper place ; nothing had been left rude or
native in him ; a well digested convention-
alism had incorporated itself thoroughly with
his substance and transformed him into

a work of art. Perhaps it was this pecu-
liarity that invested him with a species of
ghastliness and awe. It is the effect of
any thing completely and consummately
artificial, in human shape, that the person
impresses us as an unreality and as having
hardly pith enough to cast a shadow upon
the floor. As regarded Feathertop, all this
resulted in a wild, extravagant, and fantas-
tical impression, as if his life and being were
akin to the smoke that curled upward from
his pipe.

But pretty Polly Gookin felt not thus.
The pair were now promenading the room ;
Feathertop with his dainty stride and no less
dainty grimace ; the girl with a native
maidenly grace, just touched, not spoiled,
by a slightly affected manner, which seemed
caught from the perfect artifice of her companion. The longer the interview continued,
the more charmed was pretty Polly, until,
within the first quarter of an hour, (as the
old magistrate noted by his watch,) she was
evidently beginning to be in love. Nor need

it have been witchcraft that subdued her in such a hurry ; the poor child's heart, it may be, was so very fervent that it melted her with its own warmth as reflected from the hollow semblance of a lover. No matter what Feathertop said, his words found depth and reverberation in her ear ; no matter what he did, his action was heroic to her eye. And by this time it is to be supposed there was a blush on Polly's cheek, a tender smile about her mouth, and a liquid softness in her glance ; while the star kept coruscating on Feathertop's breast, and the little demons careered with more frantic merriment than ever about the circumference of his pipe-bowl. O, pretty Polly Gookin, why should these imps rejoice so madly that a silly maiden's heart was about to be given to a shadow ! Is it so unusual a misfortune, so rare a triumph ?

By and by Feathertop paused, and, throwing himself into an imposing attitude, seemed to summon the fair girl to survey his figure and resist him longer if she could.

His star, his embroidery, his buckles glowed at that instant with unutterable splendour ; the picturesque hues of his attire took a richer depth of colouring ; there was a gleam and polish over his whole presence betokening the perfect witchery of well-ordered manners. The maiden raised her eyes and suffered them to linger upon her companion with a bashful and admiring gaze. Then, as if desirous of judging what value her own simple comeliness might have side by side with so much brilliancy, she cast a glance towards the full length looking glass in front of which they happened to be standing. It was one of the truest plates in the world, and incapable of flattery. No sooner did the images therein reflected meet Polly's eye than she shrieked, shrank from the stranger's side, gazed at him for a moment in the wildest dismay, and sank insensible upon the floor, Feathertop likewise had looked towards the mirror, and there beheld, not the glittering mockery of his outside show, but a picture of the sordid patchwork of his real composition, stripped of all witchcraft.

The wretched simulacrum! We almost pity him. He threw up his arms with an expression of despair that went further than any of his previous manifestations towards vindicating his claims to be reckoned human; for, perchance the only time since this so often empty and deceptive life of mortals began its course, an illusion had seen and fully recognised itself.

III.

MOTHER RIGBY was seated by her kitchen hearth in the twilight of this eventful day, and had just shaken the ashes out of a new pipe, when she heard a hurried tramp along the road. Yet it did not seem so much the tramp of human footsteps as the clatter of sticks or the rattling of dry bones.

'Ha!' thought the old witch,' 'what step is that? Whose skeleton is out of its grave now, I wonder?'

A figure burst headlong into the cottage door. It was Feathertop! His pipe was still alight; the star still flamed upon his breast; the embroidery still glowed upon his garments; nor had he lost, in any degree or manner that could be estimated, the aspect that assimilated him with our mortal brotherhood. But yet, in some indescribable way, (as is the case with all that has deluded us when once found out,) the poor reality was felt beneath the cunning artifice.

'What has gone wrong?' demanded the witch. 'Did yonder sniffling hypocrite thrust my darling from his door? The villain! I'll set twenty fiends to torment him till he offer thee his daughter on his bended knees!'

'No, mother,' said Feathertop despondingly; 'it was not that.'

'Did the girl scorn my precious one?' asked Mother Rigby, her fierce eyes glowing like two coals of Tophet. I'll cover her face with pimples! Her nose shall be as red as the coal in my pipe! Her front teeth shall drop out!   In a week hence she shall not be worth thy having!'

'Let her alone, mother,' answered poor Feathertop; 'the girl was half won; and methinks a kiss from her sweet lips might have made me altogether human.   But,' he added, after a brief pause and then a howl of self-contempt, 'I've seen myself, mother!   I've seen myself for the wretched, ragged, empty thing I am! I'll exist no longer!'

Snatching the pipe from his mouth, he flung it with all his might against the chimney, and at the same instant sank upon the floor, a medley of straw and tattered garments, with some sticks protruding from the heap, and a shrivelled pumpkin in the midst.   The eye-holes were now lustreless; but the rudely carved gap, that just before had been a mouth, still seemed to twist itself into a despairing grin, and was so far human.

'Poor fellow!' quoth Mother Rigby, with a rueful glance at the relics of her ill-fated contrivance. 'My poor, dear, pretty Feather-top! There are thousands upon thousands of coxcombs and charlatans in the world, made up of just such a jumble of worn-out, forgotten, and good-for-nothing trash as he was! Yet they live in fair repute, and never see themselves for what they are. And why should my poor puppet be the only one to know himself and perish for it?

While thus muttering, the witch had filled a fresh pipe of tobacco, and held the stem between her fingers, as doubtful whether to thrust it into her own mouth or Feathertop's.'

'Poor Feathertop!' she continued. 'I could easily give him another chance and send him forth again to-morrow. But no; his feelings are too tender, his sensibilities too deep. He seems to have too much heart to bustle for his own advantage in such an empty and heartless world. Well! Well! I'll make a scarecrow of him after all.' 'Tis an innocent and a useful vocation, and will suit my darling well; and if each of his human brethren had as fit a one, 'twould be better for mankind;

and as for this pipe of tobacco, I need it more than he.'

So saying, Mother Rigby put the stem between her lips. 'Dickon!' cried she, in her high, sharp tone, 'another coal for my pipe!'

PASSAGES FROM A RELINQUISHED WORK.

I. AT HOME.

FROM infancy I was under the guardianship of a village parson, who made me the subject of daily prayer and the sufferer of innumerable stripes, using no distinction, as to those marks of paternal love, between myself and his own three boys. The result, it must be owned, has been very different in their cases and mine, they being all respectable men and well settled in life ; the eldest as the successor to his father's pulpit, the second as a physician, and the third as a partner in a wholesale shoe store ; while I, with better prospects than either of them, have seen the course which this present writing will describe. Yet there is room for doubt whether I should have been any better contented with such success as theirs than with my own misfortunes—at least, till after my experience of the latter had made it too late for another trial.

My guardian had a name of considerable eminence, and fitter for the place it occupies in ecclesiastical history than for so frivolous a page as mine. In his own vicinity, among the lighter part of his hearers, he was called Parson Thumpcushion, from the very forcible gestures with which he illustrated his doctrines. Certainly, if his powers as a preacher were to be estimated by the damage done to his pulpit furniture, none of his living brethren, and but few dead ones, would have been worthy even to pronounce a benediction after him. Such sounding and expounding the moment he began to grow warm, such slapping with his open palm, thumping with his closed fist, and banging with the whole weight of the great Bible, convinced me that he held, in imagination, either the old Nick, or some Unitarian infidel at bay, and belaboured his unhappy cushion as proxy for those abominable adversaries. Nothing but this exercise of the body while delivering his sermons could have supported the good parson's health under the mental toil which they cost him in composition.

Though Parson Thumpcushion had an upright heart, and some called it a warm one, he was invariably stern and severe, on principle I suppose, to me. With late justice, though early enough, even now, to be tinctured with generosity, I acknowledge him to have been a good and wise man after his own fashion. If his management failed as to myself, it succeeded with his three sons ; nor, I must frankly say, could any mode of education with which it was possible for him to be acquainted, have made me much better than what I was, or led me to a happier fortune than the present. He could neither change the nature that God gave me, nor adapt his own inflexible mind to my peculiar character. Perhaps it was my chief misfortune that I had neither father nor mother alive ; for parents have an instinctive sagacity in regard to the welfare of their children, and the child feels a confidence both in the wisdom and affection of his parents which he cannot transfer to any delegate of their duties, however conscientious. An orphan's fate is hard, be he rich or be he poor. As for Parson Thumpcushion, whenever I see the old gentleman in my dreams he looks kindly and sorrowfully at me, holding out his hand as if each had something to forgive. With such kindness and such forgiveness, but without the sorrow, may our next meeting be!

I was a youth of gay and happy temperament, with an incorrigible levity of spirit, of no vicious propensities, sensible enough, but wayward and fanciful. What a character was this to be brought into contact with the stern old Pilgrim spirit of my guardian! We were at variance on a thousand points; but our chief and final dispute arose from the pertinacity with which he insisted on my adopting a particular profession: while I, being heir to a moderate competence, had avowed my purpose of keeping aloof from the regular business of life. This would have been a dangerous resolution anywhere in the world; it was fatal in New England. There is a grossness in the conceptions of my countrymen; they will not be convinced that any good thing may consist with what they call idleness; they can anticipate nothing but evil of a young man who neither studies physic, law, nor gospel, nor opens a store, nor takes to farming, but manifests an incomprehensible disposition to be satisfied with what his father left him. The principle is excellent in its general influence, but most miserable in its effect on the few that violate it. I had a quick sensitiveness to public opinion, and felt as if it ranked me with the tavern haunters and town-paupers—with the drunken poet who hawked his own Fourth of July Odes, and the broken soldier who had been good for nothing since last war. The consequence of all this was a piece of light-hearted desperation.

I do not over-estimate my notoriety when I take it for granted that many of my readers must have heard of me in the wild way of life which I adopted. The idea of becoming a wandering story-teller had been suggested a year or two before, by an encounter with several merry vagabonds in a showman's wagon, where they and I had sheltered ourselves during a summer shower. The project was not more extravagant than most which a young man forms. Stranger ones are executed everyday; and, not to mention my prototypes in the East, and the wandering orators and poets whom my own ears have heard, I had the example of one illustrious itinerant in the other hemisphere --of Goldsmith, who planned and performed his travels through France and Italy on a less promising scheme than mine. I took credit to myself for various qualifications, mental and personal, suited to the under- taking. Besides, my mind had latterly tormented me for employment, keeping up an irregular activity even in sleep, and making me conscious that I must toil, if it were but in catching butterflies. But my chief motives were, discontent with home and a bitter grudge against Parson Thump-cushion, who would rather have laid me in my father's tomb than seen me either a novelist or an actor, two characters which I thus hit upon a method of uniting. After all, it was not half so foolish as if I had written romances instead of reciting them.

The following pages will contain a picture of my vagrant life, intermixed with speci-mens, generally brief and slight, of that great mass of fiction to which I gave exist-ence, and which has vanished like cloud shapes. Besides the occasions when I sought a pecuniary reward, I was accustomed to exercise my narrative faculty wherever chance had collected a little audience idle enough to listen. These rehearsals were useful in testing the strong points of my stories ; and, indeed, the flow of fancy soon came upon me so abundantly that its in-dulgence was its own reward, though the hope of praise also became a powerful incite-ment. Since I shall never feel the warm gush of new thought as I did then, let me beseech the reader to believe that my tales were not always so cold as he may find them now. With each specimen will be given a sketch of the circumstances in which the story was told. Thus my air-drawn pictures will be set in frames perhaps more valuable than the pictures themselves, since they will be embossed with groups of characteristic figures, amid the lake and mountain scenery, the villages and fertile fields, of our native land. But I write the book for the sake of its moral, which many a dreaming youth may profit by, though it is the experience of a wandering story-teller.

II. A FLIGHT IN THE FOG.

I set out on my rambles one morning in June about sunrise. The day promised to be fair, though at that early hour a heavy mist lay along the earth and settled in minute globules on the folds of my clothes, so that I looked precisely as though touched with a hoarfrost.

The sky was quite obscured, and the trees and houses invisible till they grew out of the fog as I came close upon them. There is a hill towards the west, whence the road goes abruptly down, holding a level course through the village and ascending an eminence on the other side, behind which it disappears. The whole view comprises an extent of half-a-mile. Here I paused; and, while gazing through the misty veil, it partially rose and swept away with so sudden an effect that a gray cloud seemed to have taken the aspect of a small white town. A thin vapour being still diffused through the atmosphere, the wreaths and pillars of fog, whether hung in air or based on earth, appeared not less substantial than the edifices, and gave their own indistinctness to the whole. It was singular that such an unromantic scene should look so visionary.

Half of the parson's dwelling was a dingy white house, and half of it was a cloud; but Squire Moody's mansion, the grandest in the village, was wholly visible, even the lattice work of the balcony under the great window; while in another place only two red chimneys were seen above the mist, appertaining to my own paternal residence, then tenanted by strangers. I could not remember those with whom I had dwelt there, not even my mother. The brick edifice of the bank was in the clouds; the foundations of what was to be a great block of buildings had vanished, ominously, as it proved; the dry-goods' store of Mr. Nightingale seemed a doubtful concern; and Dominicus Pike's tobacco manufactory an affair of smoke, except the splendid image of an Indian chief in front. The white spire of the meeting house ascended out of the densest heap of vapour, as if that shadowy base were its only support; or, to give a truer representation, the steeple was the emblem of Religion, enveloped in mystery below, yet pointing to a cloudless atmosphere, and catching the brightness of the east on its gilded vane.

As I beheld these objects, and the dewy street, with grassy intervals, and a border of trees between the wheel tracks and the side-walks, all so indistinct, and not to be traced without an effort, the whole seemed more like memory than reality. I would have imagined that years had already passed, and I was far away, contemplating that dull picture of my native place, which I should retain in my mind through the mist of time. No tears fell from my eyes among the dew-drops of the morning; nor does it occur to me that I heaved a sigh. In truth, I had never felt such a delicious excitement, nor known what freedom was till that moment when I gave up my home and took the whole world in exchange, fluttering the wings of my spirit as if I would have flown from one star to another through the universe. I waved my hand toward the dusky village, bade it a joyous farewell, and turned away to follow any path but that which might lead me back. Never was Childe Harold's sentiment adopted in a spirit more unlike his own.

Naturally enough, I thought of Don

Quixote. Recollecting how the knight and Sancho had watched for auguries when they took the road to Toboso, I began, between jest and earnest, to feel a similar anxiety. It was gratified, and by a more poetical phenomenon than the braying of the dappled ass, or the neigh of Rosinante. The sun, then just above the horizon, shone faintly through the fog, and formed a species of rainbow in the west, bestriding my intended road like a gigantic portal. I had never known before that a bow could be generated between the sunshine and the morning mist. It had no brilliancy, no perceptible hues, but was a mere unpainted framework, as white and ghostlike as the lunar rainbow, which is deemed ominous of evil. But, with a light heart to which all omens were propitious, I advanced beneath the misty archway of futurity.

I had determined not to enter on my profession within a hundred miles of home, and then to cover myself with a fictitious name. The first precaution was reasonable enough, as otherwise Parson Thumpcushion might have put an untimely catastrophe to my story; but as nobody would be much affected by my disgrace, and all was to be suffered in my own person, I know not why I cared about a name. For a week or two I travelled almost at random, seeking hardly any guidance, except the whirling of a leaf at some turn of the road, or the green bough that beckoned me, or the naked branch that pointed its withered finger onward. All my care was to be farther from home each night than the preceding morning.

III. A FELLOW TRAVELLER.

ONE day at noontide, when the sun had burst suddenly out of a cloud and threatened to dissolve me, I looked round for shelter, whether of tavern, cottage, barn, or shady tree. The first which offered itself was a wood—not a forest, but a trim plantation of young oaks, growing just thick enough to keep the mass of sunshine out, while they admitted a few straggling beams, and thus produced the most cheerful gloom imaginable. A brook, so small and clear, and apparently so cool, that I wanted to drink it up, ran under the road through a little arch of stone without once meeting the sun in its passage from the shade on one side to the shade on the other. As there was a stepping-place over the stone-wall and a path along the rivulet, I followed it and discovered its source—a spring gushing out of an old barrel.

In this pleasant spot I saw a light pack suspended from the branch of a tree, a stick leaning against the trunk, and a person seated on the grassy verge of the spring, with his back towards me. He was a slender figure, dressed in black broadcloth, which was none of the finest, nor very fashionably cut. On hearing my footsteps he started up rather nervously, and, turning round, showed the face of a young man about my own age, with his finger in a volume which he had been reading till my intrusion. His book was evidently a pocket Bible. Though I piqued myself at that period on my great penetration into people's characters and pursuits, I could not decide whether this young man in black were an unfledged divine from Andover, a college student, or preparing for College at some Academy. In either case, I would quite as willingly have found a merrier companion; such, for instance, as the comedian with whom Gil Blas shared his dinner beside a fountain in Spain.

After a nod, which was duly returned, I made a goblet of oak-leaves, filled and emptied it two or three times, and then remarked, to hit the stranger's classical associations, that this beautiful fountain ought to flow from an urn instead of an old barrel. He did not show that he understood the allusion and replied very briefly, with a shyness that was quite out of place between persons who met in such circumstances. Had he treated my next observation in the same way, we should have parted without another word.

'It is very singular,' said I,—'though doubtless there are good reasons for it,—that Nature should provide drink so abundantly, and lavish it everywhere by the roadside, but so seldom anything to eat. Why should we not find a loaf of bread on this tree as well as a barrel of good liquor at the foot of it ?'

'There is a loaf of bread on the tree,' replied the stranger, without even smiling at a coincidence which made me laugh. 'I have something to eat in my bundle ; and, if you can make a dinner with me, you shall be welcome.'

'I accept your offer with pleasure,' said I. 'A pilgrim such as I am must not refuse a providential meal.'

The young man had risen to take his bundle from the branch of the tree, but now turned round and regarded me with great earnestness, colouring deeply at the same time. However, he said nothing, and produced part of the loaf of bread and some cheese, the former being evidently home-baked, though some days out of the oven. The fare was good enough, with a real welcome, such as his appeared to be. After spreading these articles on the stump of a tree, he proceeded to ask a blessing on our food, an unexpected ceremony, and quite an impressive one at our woodland table, with the fountain gushing beside us and the bright sky glimmering through the boughs ; nor did his brief petition affect me less because his embarrassment made his voice tremble. At the end of the meal he returned thanks with the same tremulous fervour.

He felt a natural kindness for me after thus relieving my necessities, and showed it by becoming less reserved. On my part, I professed never to have relished a dinner better ; and, in requital of the stranger's hospitality, solicited the pleasure of his company to supper.

'Where ? At your home ?' asked he.

'Yes,' said I, smiling.

'Perhaps our roads are not the same,' observed he.

'O, I can take any road but one, and yet not miss my way,' answered I. 'This morning I breakfasted at home; I shall sup at home to-night; and a moment ago I dined at home. To be sure, there was a certain place which I called home; but I have resolved not to see it again till I have been quite round the globe, and enter the street on the east as I left it on the west. In the meantime, I have a home everywhere, or nowhere, just as you please to take it.'

'Nowhere then; for this transitory world is not our home,' said the young man, with solemnity. 'We are all pilgrims and wanderers; but it is strange that we two should meet.'

I inquired the meaning of this remark; but could obtain no satisfactory reply. But we had eaten salt together, and it was right that we should form acquaintance after that ceremony as the Arabs of the desert do, especially as he had learned something about myself, and the courtesy of the country entitled me to as much information in return. I asked whither he was travelling.

'I do not know,' said he; 'but God knows.'

'That is strange!' exclaimed I; 'not that God should know it, but that you should not. And how is your road to be pointed out?'

'Perhaps by my inward conviction,' he replied, looking sideways at me to discover whether I smiled; 'perhaps by an outward sign.'

'Then, believe me, 'said I, 'the outward sign is already granted you, and the inward conviction ought to follow. We are told of pious men in old times who committed themselves to the care of Providence, and saw the manifestation of its will in the slightest circumstances, as in the shooting of a star, the flight of a bird, or the course taken by some brute animal. Sometimes even a stupid ass was their guide. May not I be as good a one?'

'I do not know,' said the pilgrim, with perfect simplicity.

We did, however, follow the same road, and were not overtaken, as I partly apprehended, by the keepers of any lunatic asylum in pursuit of a stray patient.   Perhaps the stranger felt as much doubt of my sanity as I did of his, though certainly with less justice, since I was fully aware of my own extravagances, while he acted as wildly, and deemed it heavenly wisdom.   We were a singular couple, strikingly contrasted, yet curiously assimilated, each of us remarkable enough by himself, and doubly so in the other's company. Without any formal compact, we kept together day after day, till our union appeared permanent.   Even had I seen nothing to love and admire in him, I could never have thought of deserting one who needed me continually; for I never knew a person, not even a woman so unfit to roam the world in solitude as he was—so painfully shy, so easily discouraged by slight obstacles, and so often depressed by a weight within himself.

I was now far from my native place, but had not yet stepped before the public. A slight tremor seized me whenever I thought of relinquishing the immunities of a private character, and giving every man, and for money too, the right, which no man yet possessed, of treating me with open scorn. But about a week after contracting the above alliance I made my bow to an audience of nine persons, seven of whom hissed me in a very disagreeable manner, and not without good cause. Indeed, the failure was so signal that it would have been mere swindling to retain the money, which had been paid on the implied contract to give its value in amusement. So I called in the door-keeper, bade him refund the whole receipts, a mighty sum, and was gratified with a round of applause by way of offset to the hisses. This result would have looked most horrible in anticipation—a thing to make a man shoot himself, or run-a-muck, or hide himself in caverns where he might not see his own burning blush ; but the reality was not so very hard to bear. It is a fact that I was more deeply grieved by an almost parallel misfortune, which happened to my companion on the same evening. In my own behalf I was angry and excited, not depressed; my blood ran quick, my spirits rose buoyantly, and I had never felt such a confidence of future success and determination to achieve, as at that trying moment. I resolved to persevere, if it were only to wring the reluctant praise from my enemies.

Hitherto I had immensely underrated the difficulties of my idle trade; now I recognised that it demanded nothing short of my whole powers, cultivated to the utmost, and exerted with the same prodigality as if I were speaking for a great party or for the nation at large on the floor of the Capitol. No talent or attainment could come amiss; everything, indeed, was requisite,—wide observation, varied knowledge, deep thoughts, and sparkling ones; pathos and levity, and a mixture of both, like sunshine in a raindrop; lofty imagination, veiling itself in the garb of common life; and the practised art which alone could render these gifts, and more than these, available. Not that I ever hoped to be thus qualified. But my despair was no ignoble one; for, knowing the impossibility of satisfying myself, even should the world be satisfied, I did my best to overcome it; investigated the causes of every defect; and strove, with patient stubbornness, to remove them in the next attempt. It is one of my few sources of pride, that, ridiculous as the object was, I followed it up with the firmness and energy of a man.

I manufactured a great variety of plots and skeletons of tales, and kept them ready for use, leaving the filling up to the inspiration of the moment; though I cannot remember ever to have told a tale which did not vary considerably from my preconceived idea, and acquire a novelty of aspect as often as I repeated it. Oddly enough, my success was generally in proportion to the difference between the conception and accomplishment. I provided two or more commencements and catastrophes to many of the tales—a happy expedient, suggested by the double sets of sleeves and trimmings which diversified the suits in Sir Percy Shafton's wardrobe. But my best efforts had a unity, a wholeness, and a separate character that did not admit of this sort of mechanism.

***

IV. THE VILLAGE THEATRE.

ABOUT the first of September my fellow traveller and myself arrived at a country-town, where a small company of actors, on their return from a summer campaign in the British Provinces, were giving a series of dramatic exhibitions. A moderately sized hall of the tavern had been converted into a theatre. The performances that evening were : ' The Heir at Law,' and, ' No Song No Supper,' with the recitation of ' Alexander's Feast' between the play and the farce. The house was thin and dull. But the next day there appeared to be brighter prospects, the play-bills announcing at every corner, on the town pump, and—awful sacrilege !—on the

very door of the meeting house, an Unpre-
cedented Attraction! After setting forth the
ordinary entertainments of a theatre, the
public were informed, in the largest type
that the printing office could supply, that
the manager had been fortunate enough to
accomplish an engagement with the celebrated Story-teller. He would make his
first appearance that evening, and recite his
famous tale of Mr. Higginbotham's Catastrophe, which had been received with rapturous applause by audiences in all the principal cities. This outrageous flourish of
trumpets, be it known, was wholly unauthor-
ised by me, who had merely made an engagement for a single evening, without assuming
any more celebrity than the little I possessed.
As for the tale, it could hardly have been
applauded by rapturous audiences, being as
yet an unfilled plot; nor even when I stepped
upon the stage was it decided whether Mr.
Higginbotham should live or die.

In two or three places, underneath the
flaming bills which announced the Story-

teller, was pasted a small slip of paper, giving notice, in tremulous characters, of a religious meeting to be held at the school-house, where, with divine permission, Eliakim Abbott would address sinners on the welfare of their immortal souls.

In the evening, after the commencement of the tragedy of Douglas, I took a ramble through the town to quicken my ideas by active motion. My spirits were good, with a certain glow of mind which I had already learned to depend on as the sure prognostic of success. Passing a small and solitary school house, where a light was burning dimly and a few people were entering the door, I went in with them, and saw my friend Eliakim at the desk. He had collected about fifteen hearers, mostly females. Just as I entered he was beginning to pray in accents so low and interrupted that he seemed to doubt the reception of his efforts both with God and man. There was room for distrust in regard to the latter. At the conclusion of the prayer several of the little audience went out, leaving him to begin his discourse under such discouraging circumstances, added to his natural and agonising diffidence. Knowing that my presence on these occasions increased his embarrassment, I had stationed myself in a dusky place near the door, and now stole softly out.

On my return to the tavern the tragedy was already concluded; and, being a feeble one in itself, and indifferently performed, it left so much the better a chance for the Story-teller. The bar was thronged with customers, the toddy-stick keeping a continual tattoo : while in the hall there was a broad, deep, buzzing sound, with an occasional peal of impatient thunder—all symptoms of an overflowing house, and an eager audience. I drank a glass of wine and water, and stood at the side-scene conversing with a young person of doubtful sex. If a gentleman, how could he have performed the singing girl the night before in No Song No Supper ? Or, if a lady, why did she enact Young Norval, and now wear a green coat

and white pantaloons in the character of
Little Pickle?   In either case the dress was
pretty and the wearer bewitching : so that,
at the proper moment, I stepped forward
with a gay heart and a bold one : while the
orchestra played a tune that had resounded
at many a country ball, and the curtain, as it
rose, discovered something like a country
bar-room.   Such a scene was well-enough
adapted to such a tale.

The orchestra of our little theatre consisted of two fiddles and a clarionet ; but if
the whole harmony of the Tremont had been
there, it might have swelled in vain beneath
the tumult of applause that greeted me.
The good people of the town, knowing that
the world contained innumerable persons of
celebrity undreamt of by them, took it for
granted that I was one, and that their roar of
welcome was but a feeble echo of those
which had thundered around me in lofty
theatres.   Such an enthusiastic uproar was
never heard.   Each person seemed a *Bria-
reus* clapping a hundred hands, besides

keeping his feet and several cudgels in play with stamping and thumping on the floor; while the ladies flourished their white cambric handkerchiefs, intermixed with yellow and red bandanna, like the flags of different nations. After such a salutation, the celebrated Story-teller felt almost ashamed to produce so humble an affair as Mr. Higginbotham's Catastrophe.

This story was originally more dramatic than as there presented, and afforded good scope for mimicry and buffoonery, neither of which to my shame did I spare. I never knew the 'magic of a name' till I used that of Mr. Higginbotham. Often as I repeated it, there were louder bursts of merriment than those which responded to what, in my opinion, were more legitimate strokes of humour. The success of the piece was incalculably heightened by a stiff cue of horsehair, which Little Pickle, in the spirit of that mischief-loving character, had fastened to my collar, where, unknown to me, it kept making the queerest gestures of its own in correspondence with all mine. The audience, supposing that some enormous joke was appended to this long tail behind, were ineffably delighted, and gave way to such a tumult of approbation that, just as the story closed, the benches broke beneath them and left the whole row of my admirers on the floor. Even in that predicament they continued their applause. In after times, when I had grown a bitter moraliser, I took this scene for an example how much of fame is humbug; how much the meed of what our better nature blushes at; how much an accident; how much bestowed on mistaken principles; and how small and poor the remnant. From pit and boxes there was now a universal call for the Story-teller.

That celebrated personage came not when they did call for him. As I left the stage, the landlord, being also the postmaster, had given me a letter with the post-mark of my native village, and directed to my assumed name in the stiff old handwriting of Parson Thumpcushion. Doubtless he had heard of the rising renown of the Story-teller, and conjectured at once that such a nondescript luminary could be no other than his own lost ward. His epistle, though I never read it, affected me most painfully. I seemed to see the Puritanic figure of my guardian standing among the fripperies of the theatre and pointing to the players,—the fantastic and effeminate men, the painted women, the giddy girl in boy's clothes, merrier than modest,—pointing to these with solemn ridicule, and eyeing me with stern rebuke. His image was a type of the austere duty, and they of the vanities, of life.

I hastened with the letter to my chamber, and held it unopened in my hand while the applause of my buffoonery yet sounded through the theatre. Another train of thought came over me. The stern old man appeared again, but now with the gentleness of sorrow, softening his authority with love as a father might, and even bending his venerable head, as if to say that my errors had an apology in his own mistaken discipline. I strode twice across the chamber, then held the letter in the flame of the candle and beheld it consume unread. It is fixed in my mind, and was so at the time, that he had addressed me in a style of paternal wisdom, and love, and reconciliation which I could not have resisted, had I but risked the trial. The thought still haunts me that then I made my irrevocable choice between good and evil fate.

Meanwhile, as this occurrence had disturbed my mind and indisposed me to the present exercise of my profession, I left the town, in spite of a laudatory critique in the newspaper, and untempted by the liberal offers of the manager. As we walked onward, following the same road, on two such different errands, Eliakim groaned in spirit, and laboured with tears to convince me of the guilt and madness of my life.

I. THE NOTCH OF THE WHITE MOUNTAINS.

IT was now the middle of September. We had come since early sunrise from Bartlett, passing up through the Valley of the Saco, which extends between mountainous walls, sometimes with a steep ascent, but often as level as a church aisle. All that day and two preceding ones we had been loitering towards the heart of the White Mountains— those old crystal hills, whose mysterious brilliancy had gleamed upon our distant wanderings before we thought of visiting them. Height after height had risen and towered one above another till the clouds began to hang below the peaks. Down their slopes were the red pathways of the slides, those avalanches of earth, stones, and trees, which descend into the hollows, leaving vestiges of their track hardly to be effaced by the vegetation of ages. We had mountains behind us and mountains on each side, and a group of mightier ones ahead. Still our road went up along the Saco, right towards the centre of that group, as if to climb above the clouds in its passage to the further region.

In old times the settlers used to be astounded by the inroads of the northern Indians, coming down upon them from this mountain rampart through some defile known only to themselves. It is, indeed, a wondrous path. A demon, it might be fancied, or one of the Titans, was travelling up the valley, elbowing the heights carelessly aside as he passed, till at length a great mountain took its stand directly across his intended road. He tarries not for such an obstacle, but, rending it asunder a thousand feet from peak to base, discloses its treasures of hidden minerals, its sunless waters, all the secrets of the mountain's inmost heart, with a mighty fracture of rugged precipices on each side. This is the notch of the White Hills. Shame on me that I have attempted to describe it by so mean an image—feeling, as I do, that it is one of those symbolic scenes which lead the mind to the sentiment, though not to the conception, of Omnipotence.

We had now reached a narrow passage, which showed almost the appearance of having been cut by human strength and artifice in the solid rock. There was a wall of granite on each side, high and precipitous, especially on our right, and so smooth that a few evergreens could hardly find foothold enough to grow there. This is the entrance, or, in the direction we are going, the extremity, of the romantic defile of the Notch. Before emerging from it, the rattling of wheels approached behind us, and a stage coach rumbled out of the mountain, with seats on top and trunks behind, and a smart driver, in a drab greatcoat, touching the wheel horses with the whip stock, and reining-in the leaders. To my mind there was a sort of poetry in such an incident, hardly inferior to what would have accompanied the painted array of an Indian war party gliding forth from the same wild chasm. All the passengers, except a very fat lady on the back seat, had alighted. One was a mineralogist, a scientific, green-spectacled figure in black, bearing a heavy hammer, with which he did great damage to the precipices, and put the fragments in his pocket. Another was a well-dressed young man, who carried an opera-glass set in gold, and seemed to be making a quotation from some of Byron's rhapsodies on mountain scenery. There was also a trader, returning from Portland to the upper part of Vermont; and a fair young girl, with a very faint bloom, like one of those pale and delicate flowers which sometimes occur among Alpine cliffs.

They disappeared, and we followed them, passing through a deep pine forest, which for some miles allowed us to see nothing but its own dismal shade. Towards nightfall we reached a level amphitheatre, surrounded by a great rampart of hills, which shut out the sunshine long before it left the external world. It was here that we obtained our first view, except at a distance, of the principal group of mountains. They are majestic, and even awful, when contemplated in a proper mood, yet, by their breadth of base and the long ridges which support them, give the idea of immense bulk rather than of towering height. Mount Washington, indeed, looked near to heaven ; he was white with snow a mile downward, and had caught the only cloud that was sailing through the atmosphere to veil his head. Let us forget the other names of American statesmen that have been stamped upon these hills, but still call the loftiest WASHINGTON. Mountains are Earth's undecaying monuments. They must stand while she endures, and never should be consecrated to the mere great men of their own age and country, but to the mighty ones alone, whose glory is universal, and whom all time will render illustrious.

The air, not often sultry in this elevated region, nearly two thousand feet above the sea, was now sharp and cold, like that of a clear November evening in the lowlands. By morning, probably there would be a frost, if not a snowfall, on the grass and rye, and an icy surface over the standing water.   I was glad to perceive a prospect of comfortable quarters in a house which we were approaching, and of pleasant company in the guests who were assembled at the door.

We stood in front of a good substantial farm-house, of old date in that wild country. A sign over the door denoted it to be the White Mountain Post-Office—an establishment which distributes letters and newspapers to perhaps a score of persons, comprising the population of two or three townships among the hills.   The broad and weighty antlers of a deer, ' a stag of ten ' were fastened at the corner of the house ; a fox's bushy tail was nailed beneath them ; and a huge black paw lay on the ground, newly severed and still bleeding—the trophy of a bear hunt. Among several persons collected about the door-steps, the most remarkable was a sturdy mountaineer, of six feet two and corresponding bulk, with a heavy set of features, such as might be moulded on his own blacksmith's anvil, but yet indicative of mother wit and rough humour. As we appeared, he uplifted a tin trumpet four or five feet long, and blew a tremendous blast, either in honour of our arrival or to awaken an echo from the opposite hill.

Ethan Crawford's guests were of such a motley description as to form quite a picturesque group, seldom seen together except at some place like this, at once the pleasure house of fashionable tourists and the homely inn of country travellers. Among the company at the door were the mineralogist and the owner of the gold opera glass whom we had encountered in the Notch ; two Georgian gentlemen, who had chilled their southern blood that morning on the top of Mount Washington ; a physician and his wife from

Conway; a trader of Burlington, and an old squire of the Green Mountains; and two young married couples all the way from Massachusetts, on the matrimonial jaunt. Besides these strangers, the rugged county of Coos, in which we were, was represented by half-a-dozen wood cutters, who had slain a bear in the forest, and smitten off his paw.

I had joined the party, and had a moment's leisure to examine them before the echo of Ethan's blast returned from the hill. Not one, but many echoes had caught up the harsh and tuneless sound, untwisted its complicated threads, and found a thousand aerial harmonies in one stern trumpet tone. It was a distinct yet distant and dreamlike symphony of melodious instruments, as if an airy band had been hidden on the hill-side and made faint music at the summons. No subsequent trial produced so clear, delicate, and spiritual a concert as the first. A fieldpiece was then discharged from the top of a neighbouring hill, and gave birth to one long reverberation, which ran round the circle of mountains in an unbroken chain of sound and rolled away without a separate echo. After these experiments, the cold atmosphere drove us all into the house, with the keenest appetite for supper.

It did one's heart good to see the great fires that were kindled in the parlour and bar-room, especially the latter, where the fireplace was built of rough stone, and might have contained the trunk of an old tree for a backlog. A man keeps a comfortable hearth when his own forest is at his very door. In the parlour, when the evening was fairly set in, we held our hands before our eyes to shield them from the ruddy glow, and began a pleasant variety of conversation. The mineralogist and the physician talked about the invigorating qualities of the mountain air, and its excellent effect on Ethan Crawford's father, an old man of seventy-five, with the unbroken frame of middle life. The two brides and the doctor's wife held a whispered discussion, which, by their frequent titterings and a blush or two, seemed to have reference to the trials or enjoyments of the matrimonial state. The bridegrooms sat together in a corner, rigidly silent, like Quakers whom the spirit moveth not, being still in the odd predicament of bashfulness toward their own young wives. The Green Mountain squire chose me for his companion, and described the difficulties he had met with half a century ago in travelling from the Connecticut River through the Notch to Conway, now a single day's journey, though it had cost him eighteen. The Georgians held the Album between them, and favoured us with the few specimens of its contents, which they considered ridiculous enough to be worth hearing. One extract met with deserved applause. It was a ' Sonnet to the snow on Mount Washington,' and had been contributed that very afternoon, bearing a signature of great distinction in magazines and annuals. The lines were elegant and full of fancy, but too remote from familiar sentiment, and cold as their subject, resembling those curious specimens of crystallised vapour, which I observed next day on the mountain top. The poet was understood to be the young gentleman of the opera glass, who heard our laudatory remarks with the composure of a veteran.

Such was our party, and such their ways of amusement. But on a winter evening another set of guests assembled on the hearth where these summer travellers were now sitting. I once had it in contemplation to spend a month hereabouts, in sleighing time, for the sake of studying the yeomen of New England, who then elbow each other through the Notch by hundreds, on their way to Portland. There could be no better school for such a purpose than Ethan Crawford's inn. Let the student go thither in December, sit down with the teamsters at their meals, share their evening merriment, and repose with them at night when every bed has its three occupants, and parlour, and bed-room, bar-room, and kitchen are strewn with slumberers around the fire. Then let him rise before daylight, button his great coat, muffle up his ears, and stride with the departing caravan a mile or two, to see how sturdily they make head against the blast. A treasure of characteristic traits will repay all inconveniences, even should a frozen nose be of the number.

The conversation of our party soon became more animated and sincere, and we recounted some traditions of the Indians, who believed that the father and mother of their race were saved from a deluge by ascending the peak of Mount Washington. The children of that pair have been overwhelmed and have found no such refuge. In the mythology of the savage, these mountains were afterwards considered sacred and inaccessible, full of unearthly wonders, illuminated at lofty heights by the blaze of precious stones, and inhabited by deities, who sometimes shrouded themselves in the snow storm and came down on the lower world. There are few legends more poetical than that of 'The Great Carbuncle' of the White Mountains. The belief was communicated to the English settlers, and is hardly yet extinct, that a gem of such immense size as to be seen shining miles away, hangs from a rock over a clear, deep lake, high up among the hills. They who had once beheld its splendour were enthralled with an unutterable yearning to possess it. But a spirit guarded that inestimable jewel, and bewildered the adventurer with a dark mist from the enchanted lake. Thus life was worn away in the vain search for an unearthly treasure, till at length the deluded one went up the mountain, still sanguine as in youth, but returned no more. On this theme, methinks, I could frame a tale with a deep moral.

The hearts of the palefaces would not thrill to these superstitions of the red men, though we spoke of them in the centre of their haunted region. The habits and sentiments of that departed people were too distinct from those of their successors to find much real sympathy. It has often been a matter of regret to me that I was shut out from the most peculiar field of American fiction by an inability to see any romance or poetry, or grandeur, or beauty in the Indian character, at least till such traits were pointed out by others. I do abhor an Indian story. Yet no writer can be more secure of a permanent place in our literature than the biographer of the Indian chiefs. His subject, as referring to tribes which have mostly vanished from the earth, gives him a right to be placed on a classic shelf, apart from the merits which will sustain him there.

I made inquiries whether, in his researches about these parts, our mineralogist had found the three 'Silver Hills,' which an Indian Sachem sold to an Englishman nearly two hundred years ago, and the treasure of which the posterity of the purchaser have been looking for ever since. But the man of science had ransacked every hill along the Saco, and knew nothing of those prodigious piles of wealth. By this time, as usual with men on the eve of great adventure, we had prolonged our session deep into the night, considering how early we were to set out on our six miles' ride to the foot of Mount Washington. There was now a general breaking-up. I scrutinised the faces of the two bridegrooms, and saw but little probability of their leaving the bosom of earthly bliss, in the first week of the honeymoon and at the frosty hour of three, to climb above the clouds ; nor, when I felt how sharp the wind was as it rushed through a broken pane, and eddied between the chinks of my unplastered chamber, did I anticipate much alacrity on my own part, though we were to seek for ' The Great Carbuncle.'

II. THE CANAL BOAT.

I was inclined to be poetical about the Grand Canal. In my imagination, DeWitt Clinton was an enchanter, who had waved his magic wand from the Hudson to Lake Erie and united them by a watery highway, crowded with the commerce of two worlds, till then inaccessible to each other. This simple and mighty conception had conferred inestimable value on spots which Nature seemed to have thrown carelessly into the great body of the earth, without foreseeing that they could ever attain importance. I pictured the surprise of the sleepy Dutchmen when the new river first glittered by their doors, bringing them hard cash or foreign commodities in exchange for their hitherto unmarketable produce. Surely the water of this canal must be the most fertilising of all fluids ; for it causes towns, with their masses of brick and stone, their churches and theatres, their business and hubbub, their luxury and refinement, their gay dames and polished citizens, to spring up, till in time the wondrous stream may flow between two continuous lines of buildings, through one thronged street from Buffalo to Albany. I embarked about thirty miles below Utica, determining to voyage along the whole extent of the canal at least twice in the course of the summer.

Behold us, then, fairly afloat, with three horses harnessed to our vessel, like the steeds of Neptune to a huge scallop shell in mythological pictures. Bound to a distant port, we had neither chart nor compass, nor cared about the wind, nor felt the heaving of a billow, nor dreaded shipwreck, however fierce the tempest, in our adventurous navigation of an interminable puddle; for a mud puddle it seemed, and as dark and turbid as if every kennel in the land paid contribution to it. With an imperceptible current, it holds its drowsy way through all the dismal swamps and unimpressive scenery that could be found between the great lakes and the sea coast. Yet there is variety enough, both on the surface of the canal and along its banks, to amuse the traveller, if an overpowering tedium did not deaden his perceptions.

Sometimes we met a black and rusty-looking vessel, laden with lumber, salt from Syracuse, or Genesee flour, and shaped at both ends like a square-toed boot, as if it had two sterns, and were fated always to advance backward. On its deck would be a square hut, and a woman seen through the window at her household work, with a little tribe of children who perhaps had been born in this strange dwelling and knew no other home. Thus, while the husband smoked his pipe at the helm, and the eldest son rode one of the horses, on went the family, travelling hundreds of miles in their own house, and carrying their fireside with them. The most frequent species of craft were the ' line boats,' which had a cabin at each end, and a great bulk of barrels, bales, and boxes in the midst, or light packets like our own, decked all over with a row of curtained windows from stem to stern, and a drowsy face at every one. Once we encountered a boat of rude construction, painted all in gloomy black, and manned by three Indians, who gazed at us in silence and with a singular fixedness of eye. Perhaps these three alone, among the ancient possessors of the land, had attempted to derive benefit from the white man's mighty projects and float along in the current of his enterprise. Not long after, in the midst of a swamp and beneath a clouded sky, we overtook a vessel that seemed full of mirth and sunshine. It contained a little colony of Swiss on their way to Michigan, clad in garments of strange fashion and gay colours, scarlet, yellow, and bright blue, singing, laughing, and making merry in odd tones, and a babble of outlandish words. One pretty damsel, with a beautiful pair of naked white arms, addressed a mirthful remark to me. She spoke in her native tongue, and I retorted in good English, both of us laughing heartily at each other's unintelligible wit. I cannot describe how pleasantly this incident affected me. These honest Swiss were an itinerant community of jest and fun journeying through a gloomy land and among a dull race of money-getting drudges, meeting none to understand their mirth, and only one to sympathise with it, yet still retaining the happy lightness of their own spirit.

Had I been on my feet at the time, instead of sailing slowly along in a dirty canal boat, I should often have paused to contemplate the diversified panorama along the banks of the canal. Sometimes the scene was a forest, dark, dense, and impervious, breaking away occasionally and receding from a lonely tract, covered with dismal black stumps, where, on the verge of the canal, might be seen a log cottage and a sallow-faced woman at the window. Lean and aguish, she looked like poverty personified, half clothed, half fed, and dwelling in a desert, while a tide of wealth was sweeping by her door. Two or three miles farther would bring us to a lock, where the slight impediment to navigation had created a little mart of trade. Here would be found commodities of all sorts, enumerated in yellow letters on the window shutters of a small grocery store, the owner of which had set his soul to the gathering of coppers and small change, buying and selling through the week, and counting his gains on the blessed Sabbath. The next scene might be the dwelling houses and stores of a thriving village, built of wood or small grey stones, a church-spire rising in the midst, and generally two taverns, bearing over their piazzas the pompous titles of 'hotel,' 'exchange,' 'tontine,' or 'coffee house.' Passing on, we glide now into the unquiet heart of an inland city,—of

Utica, for instance,—and find ourselves amid piles of brick, crowded docks and quays, rich warehouses, and a busy population. We feel the eager and hurrying spirit of the place, like a stream and eddy whirling us along with it. Through the thickest of the tumult goes the canal, flowing between lofty rows of buildings and arched bridges of hewn stone. Onward, also, go we, till the hum and bustle of struggling enterprise die away behind us, and we are threading an avenue of the ancient woods again.

This sounds not amiss in description, but was so tiresome in reality that we were driven to the most childish expedients for amusement. An English traveller paraded the deck, with a rifle in his walking stick, and waged war on squirrels and woodpeckers, sometimes sending a successful bullet among flocks of tame ducks and geese which abound in the dirty water of the canal. I, also, pelted these foolish birds with apples, and smiled at the ridiculous earnestness of their scrambles for the prize while the apple bobbed about like a thing of life. Several little incidents afforded us good-natured diversion. At the moment of changing horses the tow rope caught a Massachusetts farmer by the leg and threw him down in a very indescribable posture, leaving a purple mark around his sturdy limb. A new passenger fell flat on his back in attempting to step on deck as the boat emerged from under a bridge. Another, in his Sunday clothes, as good luck would have it, being told to leap aboard from the bank, forthwith plunged up to his third waistcoat button in the canal, and was fished out in a very pitiable plight, not at all amended by the three rounds of applause. Anon, a Virginia schoolmaster, too intent on a pocket Virgil to heed the helmsman's warning ' Bridge ! bridge !' was saluted by the said bridge on his knowledge box. I had prostrated myself like a pagan before his idol, but heard the dull, leaden sound of the contact, and fully expected to see the treasures of the poor man's cranium scattered about the deck. However, as there was no harm done, except a large bump on the head, and probably a corresponding dent in the bridge, the rest of us exchanged glances, and laughed quietly. O, how pitiless are idle people.

.   .   .   .   .   .

The table being now lengthened through the cabin and spread for supper, the next twenty minutes were the pleasantest I had spent on the canal, the same space at dinner excepted. At the close of the meal it had become dusky enough for lamplight. The rain pattered unceasingly on the deck, and sometimes came with a sudden rush against the windows, driven by the wind as it stirred through an opening of the forest. The intolerable dulness of the scene engendered an evil spirit in me. Perceiving that the Englishman was taking notes in a memorandum book, with occasional glances round the cabin, I presumed that we were all to figure in a future volume of travels, and amused my ill-humour by falling into the probable vein of his remarks. He would hold up an imaginary mirror, wherein our reflected faces would appear ugly and ridiculous, yet still retain an undeniable likeness to the originals. , Then, with more sweeping malice, he would make these caricatures the representatives of great classes of my countrymen.

He glanced at the Virginia schoolmaster, a Yankee by birth, who, to recreate himself, was examining a freshman from Schenectady College in the conjugation of a Greek verb. Him the Englishman would portray as the scholar of America, and compare his erudition to a schoolboy's Latin theme made up of scraps ill-selected and worse put together. Next the tourist looked at the Massachusetts farmer, who was delivering a dogmatic harangue on the iniquity of Sunday mails. Here was the far-famed Yeoman of New England ; his religion, writes the Englishman, is gloom on the Sabbath, long prayers every morning and eventide, and illiberality at all times ; his boasted information is merely an abstract and compound of newspaper para- graphs, congress debates, caucus harangues, and the argument and judge's charge in his own law-suits.   The book-monger cast his eye at a Detroit merchant, and began scribbling faster than ever. In this sharp-eyed man, this lean man, of wrinkled brow, we see daring enterprise and close-fisted avarice combined. Here is the worshipper of Mammon at noonday ; here is the three times bankrupt, richer after every ruin ; here in one word (O wicked Englishman to say it!), here is the American. He lifted his eye-glass to inspect a western lady, who at once became aware of the glance, reddened, and retired deeper into the female part of the cabin.   Here was the pure, modest, shrinking woman of America,—shrinking when no evil is intended, and sensitive like diseased flesh, that thrills if you but point at it ; and strangely modest, without confidence in the modesty of other people ; and admirably pure, with such a quick apprehension of all impurity.

In this manner I went through all the cabin, hitting everybody as hard a lash as I could, and laying the whole blame on the infernal Englishman.   At length I caught the eyes of my own image in the looking-glass, where a number of the party were likewise reflected, and among them the Englishman, who at that moment was intensely observing myself.

The crimson curtain being let down between the ladies and gentlemen, the cabin became a bedchamber for twenty persons, who were laid on shelves one above another. For a long time our various incommodities kept us all awake except five or six, who were accustomed to sleep nightly amid the uproar of their own snoring, and had little to dread from any other species of disturbance. It is a curious fact that these snorers had been the most quiet people in the boat while awake, and became peace-breakers only when others cease to be so, breathing tumult out of their repose. Would it were possible to affix a wind instrument to the nose, and thus make melody of a snore, so that a sleepy lover might serenade his mistress, or a congregation snore a psalm tune! Other, though fainter, sounds than these contributed to my restlessness. My head was close to the crimson curtain,—the sexual division of the boat,— behind which I continually hear whispers and stealthy footsteps ; the noise of a comb laid on the table, or of a slipper dropped on the floor ; the twang, like a broken harpstring, caused by loosening a tight belt ; the rustling of a gown in its descent ; and the unlacing of a pair of stays. My ears seemed to have the properties of an eye ; a visible image pestered my fancy in the darkness ; the curtain was withdrawn between me and the western lady, who yet disrobed herself without a blush.

Finally, all was hushed in that quarter. Still I was more broad awake than through the whole preceding day, and felt a feverish impulse to toss my limbs miles apart and appease the unquietness of mind by that of matter. Forgetting that my berth was hardly so wide as a coffin, I turned suddenly over, and fell like an avalanche on the floor, to the disturbance of the whole community of sleepers. As there were no bones broken, I blessed the accident and went on deck. A lantern was burning at each end of the boat, and one of the crew was stationed at the bows, keeping watch, as mariners do on the ocean. Though the rain had ceased, the sky was all one cloud, and the darkness so intense that there seemed to be no world except the little space on which our lanterns glimmered. Yet it was an impressive scene.

We were traversing the 'long level,' a dead flat between Utica and Syracuse, where the canal has not rise or fall enough to require a lock for nearly seventy miles. There can hardly be a more dismal tract of country. The forest which covers it, consisting chiefly of white cedar, black ash, and other trees that live in excessive moisture, is now decayed and deathstruck by the partial draining of the swamp into the great ditch of the canal. Sometimes, indeed, our lights were reflected from pools of stagnant water which stretched far in among the trunks of the trees, beneath dense masses of dark foliage. But, generally, the tall stems and intermingled branches were naked, and brought into strong relief amid the surrounding gloom by the whiteness of their decay. Often we beheld the prostrate form of some old sylvan giant which had fallen and crushed down smaller trees under its immense ruin. In spots where destruction had been riotous, the lanterns showed perhaps a hundred trunks, erect, half overthrown, extended along the ground, resting on their shattered limbs or tossing them desperately into the darkness, but all of one ashy white, all naked together, in desolate confusion. Thus growing out of the night as we drew nigh, and vanishing as we glided on, based on obscurity, and overhung and bounded by it, the scene was ghostlike—the very land of unsubstantial things, whither dreams might betake themselves when they quit the slumberer's brain.

My fancy found another emblem. The wild nature of America had been driven to this desert place by the encroachments of civilised man. And even here, where the savage queen was throned on the ruins of her empire, did we penetrate, a vulgar and worldly throng, intruding on her latest solitude. In other lands, decay sits among fallen palaces; but here her home is among the forests.

Looking ahead, I discerned a distant light, announcing the approach of another boat, which soon passed us, and proved to be a rusty old scow—just such a craft as the 'Flying Dutchman' would navigate on the canal. Perhaps it was that celebrated personage himself whom I imperfectly distinguished at the helm, in a glazed cap and rough greatcoat, with a pipe in his mouth, leaving the fumes of tobacco a hundred yards behind. Shortly after, our boatman blew a horn, sending a long and melancholy note through the forest avenue, as a signal for some watcher in the wilderness to be ready with a change of horses. We had proceeded a mile or two with our fresh team, when the tow-rope got entangled in a fallen branch on the edge of the canal, and caused a momentary delay, during which I went to examine the phosphoric light of an old tree a little within the forest. It was not the first delusive radiance that I had followed.

The tree lay along the ground, and was wholly converted into a mass of diseased splendour, which threw a ghastliness around. Being full of conceits that night, I called it a frigid fire, a funeral light, illumining decay and death, an emblem of fame that gleams around the dead man without warming him, or of genius when it owes its brilliancy to moral rottenness, and was thinking that such ghostlike torches were just fit to light up this dead forest, or to blaze coldly in tombs, when, starting from my abstraction, I looked up the canal. I recollected myself, and discovered the lanterns glimmering far away.

'Boat ahoy!' shouted I, making a trumpet of my closed fists.

Though the cry must have rung for miles along that hollow passage of the woods, it produced no effect. These packet boats make up for their snail-like pace by never loitering day nor night, especially for those who have paid their fare. Indeed, the captain had an interest in getting rid of me; for I was his creditor for a breakfast.

'They are gone, Heaven be praised?' ejaculated I; 'for I cannot possibly overtake them. Here am I, on the 'long level' at midnight, with the comfortable prospect of a walk to Syracuse, where my baggage will be left. And now to find a house or shed wherein to pass the night.' So thinking aloud, I took a flambeau from the old tree, burning, but consuming not, to light my steps withal, and, like a Jack-o'-lantern, set out on my midnight tour.

GOODMAN Duston and his wife, somewhat less than a century and a half ago, dwelt in Haverhill, at that time a small frontier settlement in the province of Massachusetts Bay. They had already added seven children to the king's liege subjects in America ; and Mrs. Duston, about a week before the period of our narrative, had blessed her husband with an eighth. One day in March 1698, when Mr. Duston had gone forth about his ordinary business, there fell out an event, which had nearly left him a childless man and a widower besides. An Indian war-party, after traversing the trackless forest all the way from Canada, broke in upon their remote and defenceless town. Goodman Duston heard the war whoop and alarm ; and, being on horseback, immediately set off full speed to look after the safety of his family. As he dashed along, he beheld dark wreaths of smoke eddying from the roof of several dwellings near the road side ; while the groans of dying men, the shrieks of affrighted women, and the screams of children pierced his ear, all mingled with the horrid yell of the raging savages. The poor man trembled, yet spurred on so much the faster, dreading that he should find his cottage in a blaze, his wife murdered in her bed, and his little ones tossed into the flames. But drawing near the door, he saw his seven little children, of all ages between two years and seventeen, issuing out together, and running down the road to meet him. The father only bade them make the best of their way to the nearest garrison, and, without a moment's pause, flung himself from his horse, and rushed into Mrs. Duston's bedchamber.

The good woman, as we have before hinted, had lately added an eighth to the seven former proofs of her conjugal affection ;

and she now lay with the infant in her arms, and her nurse, the widow Mary Neff, watching by her bedside. Such was Mrs. Duston's helpess state, when her pale and breathless husband burst into the chamber, bidding her instantly to rise and flee for her life. Scarcely were the words out of his mouth, when the Indian yell was heard ; and, staring wildly out of the window, Goodman Duston saw that the bloodthirsty foe was close at hand. At this terrible instant, it appears that the thought of his children's danger rushed so powerfully upon his heart, that he quite forgot the still more perilous situation of his wife ; or, as is not improbable, he had such knowledge of the good lady's character, as afforded him a comfortable hope that she would hold her own even in a contest with a whole tribe of Indians. However that might be, he seized his gun and rushed out of doors again, meaning to gallop after his seven children, and snatch up one of them in his flight, lest his whole race and generation should be blotted from

the earth in that fatal hour. With this idea, he rode up behind them, swift as the wind. They had, by this time, got about forty rods from the house, all pressing forward in a group ; and though the younger children tripped and stumbled, yet the elder ones were not prevailed upon, by the fear of death, to take to their heels and leave these poor little souls to perish. Hearing the tramp of hoofs in their rear, they looked round, and copying Goodman Duston, all suddenly stopped. The little ones stretched out their arms ; while the elder boys and girls, as it were, resigned their charge into his hands ; and all the seven children seemed to say :—
' Here is our father ! Now we are safe !'

But if ever a poor mortal was in trouble, and perplexity, and anguish of spirit, that man was Mr. Duston. He felt his heart yearn towards these seven helpless children, as if each were singly possessed of his whole affections ; for not one among them all, but had some peculiar claim to their father's love. There was his first born ; there, too, the little one, who, till within a week past, had been the baby; there was a girl with her mother's features, and a boy the picture of himself, and another in whom the looks of both parents were mingled; there was one child, whom he loved for his mild, quiet, and holy disposition, and had destined him to be a minister; and another, whom he loved not less for his rough and fearless spirit, and who, could he live to be a man, would do a man's part against these bloody Indians. Goodman Duston looked at the poor things, one by one; and, with yearning fondness, he looked at them all together; then he gazed up to Heaven for a moment, and finally waved his hand to his seven beloved ones. 'Go on, my children,' said he, calmly, 'we will live or die together!'

He reined-in his horse, and caused him to walk behind the children, who, hand in hand, went onward, hushing their sobs and wailings, lest these sounds should bring the savages upon them. Nor was it long before the fugitives had proof that the red devils had found their track. There was a curl of smoke from behind the huge trunk of a tree -a sudden and sharp report echoed through the woods—and a bullet hissed over Goodman Duston's shoulder, and passed over the children's heads. The father, turning half round on his horse, took aim and fired at the skulking foe, with such effect as to cause a momentary delay of the pursuit. Another shot—and another—whistled from the covert of the forest ; but still the little band pressed on unharmed ; and the stealthy nature of the Indians forbade them to rush boldly forward, in the face of so firm an enemy as Goodman Duston. Thus he and his seven children continued their retreat, creeping along, 'at the pace of a child five years old,' till the stockades of a little frontier fortress appeared in view, and the savages gave up the chase.

We must not forget Mrs. Duston in her distress. Scarcely had her husband fled from the house, ere the chamber was thronged with the horrible visages of the wild Indians, bedaubed with paint and besmeared with blood, brandishing their tomahawks in her face, and threatening to add her scalp to those that were already hanging at their girdles. It was, however, their interest to save her alive, if the thing might be, in order to exact a ransom. Our great-great-grandmothers, when taken captive in the old times of Indian warfare, appear, in nine cases out of ten, to have been in pretty much such a delicate situation as Mrs. Duston; notwithstanding which, they were wonderfully sustained through long, rough, and hurried marches, amid toil, weariness, and starvation, such as the Indians themselves could hardly endure. Seeing that there was no help for it, Mrs. Duston rose, and she and the widow Neff, with the infant in her arms, followed their captors out of doors. As they crossed the threshold, the poor babe sent up a feeble wail; it was its death-cry. In an instant, an Indian seized it by the heels, swung it in the air, dashed out its brains against the trunk of the nearest tree, and threw the little corpse at the mother's feet. Perhaps it was the remembrance of that moment, that hardened Hannah Duston's heart, when her time of vengeance came. But now, nothing could be done but to stifle her grief and rage within her bosom, and follow the Indians into the dark gloom of the forest, hardly venturing to throw a parting glance at the blazing cottage, where she had dwelt happily with her husband, and had borne him eight children— the seven, of whose fate she knew nothing, and the infant, whom she had just seen murdered.

The first day's march was fifteen miles; and during that, and many succeeding days, Mrs. Duston kept pace with her captors; for, had she lagged behind, a tomahawk would at once have been sunk into her brains. More than one terrible warning was given her; more than one of her fellow-captives, of whom there were many, after tottering feebly, at length sank upon the ground. The next moment the death groan was breathed, and the scalp was reeking at the Indian's girdle. The unburied corpse was left in the forest, till the rites of sepulture should be performed by the autumnal gales strewing the withered leaves upon the whitened bones. When out of danger of immediate pursuit, the prisoners, according to Indian custom, were divided among different parties of the savages, each of whom were to shift for themselves. Mrs. Duston, the widow Neff, and an English lad, fell to the lot of a family consisting of two stout warriors, three squaws, and seven children. These Indians, like most with whom the French had held intercourse, were Catholics ; and, on Mrs. Duston's authority, it is affirmed that they prayed at morning, noon, and night, nor ever partook of food without a prayer, nor suffered their children to sleep, till they had prayed to the Christian's God. Cotton Mather, like an old hard-hearted, pedantic bigot as he was, seems trebly to exult in the destruction of these poor wretches on account of their Popish superstitions. Yet what can be more touching than to think of these wild Indians, in their loneliness and their wanderings, wherever they went among the dark, mysterious woods, still keeping up domestic worship, with all the regularity of a household at its peaceful fireside.

They were travelling to a rendezvous of the savages, somewhere in the north-east. One night, being now above a hundred miles from Haverhill, the red men and women, and the little red children, and the three pale-faces, Mrs. Duston, the widow Neff, and the English lad, made their encampment, and kindled a fire beneath the gloomy old trees on a small island in Contocook river. The barbarians sat down to what scanty food Providence had sent them, and shared it with their prisoners, as if they had all been the children of one wigwam, and had grown up together on the margin of the same river within the shadow of the forest. Then the Indians said their prayers,—the prayers that the Romish priests had taught them,—and made the sign of the cross upon their dusky breasts, and composed themselves to rest. But the three prisoners prayed apart ; and,

when their petitions were ended, they likewise lay down with their feet to the fire.
The night wore on, and the light and
cautious slumbers of the red men were often
broken by the rush and ripple of the stream,
or the groaning and moaning of the forest, as
if nature were wailing over her wild children;
and sometimes, too, the little redskins cried in
their sleep, and the Indian mothers awoke to
hush them. But a little before break of day,
a dead, deep slumber fell upon the Indians.

Up rose Mrs. Duston, holding her own
breath to listen to the long deep breathings
of her captors. Then she stirred the widow
Neff, whose place was by her own, and likewise the English lad, and all three stood up,
with the doubtful gleam of the decaying fire
hovering upon their ghastly visages as they
stared round at the fated slumberers. The
next moment each of the three captives held
a tomahawk. Hark! that low moan, as of
one in a troubled dream; it told a warrior's
death pang. Another! Another! and the
third half-uttered groan was from a woman's

lips. But oh! the children. Their skins are red, yet spare them; Hannah Duston, spare these seven little ones, for the sake of the seven that have fed at your own breast! 'Seven,' quoth Mrs. Duston to herself. 'Eight children have I borne, and where are the seven, and where is the eighth?' The thought nerved her arm; and the copper-coloured babes slept the same dead sleep with their Indian mothers. Of all that family, only one woman escaped, dreadfully wounded, and fled shrieking into the wilderness; and a boy, whom, it is said, Mrs. Duston had meant to save alive. But he did well to flee from the raging tigress! There was little safety for a redskin when Hannah Duston's blood was up.

The work being finished, Mrs. Duston laid hold of the long black hair of the warriors, and the women, and the children, and took all their ten scalps, and left the island, which bears her name to this day. According to our notion it should be held accursed for her sake. Would that the bloody old hag had been drowned in crossing Contocook river, or that she had sunk over head and ears in a swamp, and been there buried, till summoned forth to confront her victims at the day of judgment; or that she had gone astray and been starved to death in the forest, and nothing ever seen of her again, save her skeleton with the ten scalps twisted round it for a girdle! But, on the contrary, she and her companions came safe home, and received the bounty on the dead Indians, besides liberal presents from private gentlemen, and fifty pounds from the Governor of Maryland. In her old age, being sunk into decayed circumstances, she claimed, and we believe received, a pension, as a further price of blood.

This awful woman and that tender-hearted man, her husband, will be remembered as long as the deeds of old times are told round a New England fireside. But how different is her renown from his!

It is a curious fact, that the custom of making April fools prevails in the most widely separated regions of the globe, and that, everywhere, its origin is hidden in remote antiquity. The Hindoos on the Ganges practise it; in all the European countries it exists, in one shape or another; the French make what they call April Fish; and, in America, it is one of the few mirthful customs brought from merry old England. When once such a fashion was established, we should suppose that human nature might be pretty safely trusted to keep it up. It is desirable to have the privilege of saying, on one day in the year—what we perhaps think everyday—that our acquaintances are fools. But the false refinement of the present age has occasioned the rites of the holiday to fall into desuetude. It is not unreasonable to conjecture, that this child's play, as it has now become, was, when originally instituted, a vehicle for the strongest satire which mankind could wreak upon itself. The people of antiquity, we may imagine, used to watch each other's conduct throughout the year, and assemble on All Fools' Day, to pass judgment on what they had observed. Whoever, in any respect, had gone astray from reason and common sense, the community were licensed to point the finger, and laugh at them for an April fool. How many, we wonder, whether smooth-chinned or grey-bearded, would be found so wise in great and little matters, as to escape the pointed finger and the laugh.

It is a pity that this excellent old custom has so degenerated. Much good might still result from such a festival of foolery; for, though our own individual follies are too intimately blended with our natures to be seen or felt, yet the dullest of us are sufficiently acute in detecting the foolery of our neighbours. Let us, by way of example, point our finger at a few of the sage candidates for the honours of All Fools' day.

He who has wasted the past year in idleness, neglecting his opportunities of honourable exertion; he who has learnt nothing good, nor weeded his mind of anything evil; he who has been heaping up gold, and thereby gained as many cares and inquietudes as there are coins in his strong box; he who has reduced himself from affluence to poverty, whether by riotous living or desperate speculations; these four are April fools. He who has climbed, or suffered himself to be lifted, to a station for which he is unfit, does but stand upon a pedestal, to show the world an April fool. The grey-haired man, who has sought the joys of wedlock with a girl in her teens, and the young girl who has wedded an old man for his wealth, are a pair of April fools. The married couple, who have linked themselves for life, on the strength of a week's liking; the ill-matched pair, who turn their roughest sides toward each other, instead of making the best of a bad bargain ; the young man who has doomed himself to a life of difficulties by a too early marriage; the middle-aged bachelor, who is waiting to be rich ; the damsel who has trusted her lover too far; the lover who is downcast for a damsel's fickleness—all these are April fools. The farmer, who has left a good homestead in New England, to emigrate to the Mississippi valley, or anywhere else, on this side of heaven ; the fresh-cheeked youth, who has gone to find his grave at New Orleans ; the Yankees, who have enlisted for Texas ; the merchant, who has speculated on a French war ; the author who writes for fame—or for bread, if he can do better ; the student, who has turned aside from the path of his profession, and gone astray in poetry and fancifulness :—what are these but a motley group of April fools ? And the wiseacre, who thinks himself a fool in nothing—Oh, superlative April fool !

But what a fool are we, to waste our ink and paper in making out a catalogue of April fools. We will add but one or two more. He who, for any earthly consideration, inflicts a wrong on his own conscience, is a most egregious April fool. The mortal man, who has neglected to think of eternity, till he finds himself at the utmost bourne of Time,—Death points at him for an April fool. And now let the whole world, discerning its own nonsense, and humbug, and charlatanism, and how in all things, or most, it is both a deceiver and deceived—let it point its innumerable fingers, and shout in its own ear, ' O world, you April fool!' Lastly, if the reader in turning over this page, has not profited by the moral truths which it contains, must we not write him down in our list of April fools ? But if there be no truth, nothing well said, nor worth saying, we shall find it out anon ; and whisper to ourself, ' Mr. Author, you are an April fool.'

THE other day, having a leisure hour at my disposal, I stepped into a new museum, to which my notice was casually drawn by a small and unobtrusive sign: 'TO BE SEEN HERE A VIRTUOSO'S COLLECTION.' Such was the simple yet not altogether unpromising announcement that turned my steps aside for a little while from the sunny side-walk of our principal thoroughfare. Mounting a sombre staircase, I pushed open a door at its summit, and found myself in the presence of a person, who mentioned the moderate sum that would entitle me to admittance.

'Three shillings, Massachusetts tenor,' said he. 'No, I mean half a dollar, as you reckon in these days.'

While searching my pocket for the coin I

glanced at the doorkeeper, the marked character and individuality of whose aspect encouraged me to expect something not quite in the ordinary way. He wore an old-fashioned great-coat, much faded, within which his meagre form was so completely enveloped that the rest of his attire was undistinguishable. But his visage was remarkably wind-flushed, sunburnt, and weather-worn, and had a most unquiet, nervous, and apprehensive expression. It seemed as if this man, had some all-important object in view, some point of deepest interest to be decided, some momentous question to ask, might he but hope for a reply. As it was evident, however, that I could have nothing to do with his private affairs, I passed through an open doorway, which admitted me into the extensive hall of the museum.

Directly in front of the portal was the bronze statue of a youth with winged feet. He was represented in the act of flitting away from earth, yet wore such a look of earnest invitation that it impressed me like a summons to enter the hall.

'It is the original statue of Opportunity, by the ancient sculptor Lysippus,' said a gentleman who now approached me. 'I place it at the entrance of my museum, because it is not at all times that one can gain admittance to such a collection.'

The speaker was a middle-aged person, of whom it was not easy to determine whether he had spent his life as a scholar or as a man of action ; in truth, all outward and obvious peculiarities had been worn away by an extensive and promiscuous intercourse with the world. There was no mark about him of profession, individual habits, or scarcely of country ; although his dark complexion and high features made me conjecture that he was a native of some southern clime of Europe. At all events, he was evidently the Virtuoso in person.

'With your permission,' said he, 'as we have no descriptive catalogue, I will accompany you through the museum and point out whatever may be most worthy of attention.

In the first place, here is a choice collection of stuffed animals.'

Nearest the door stood the outward semblance of a wolf, exquisitely prepared, it is true, and showing a very wolfish fierceness in the large glass eyes which were inserted into its wild and crafty head. Still it was merely the skin of a wolf, with nothing to distinguish it from other individuals of that unlovely breed.

'How does this animal deserve a place in your collection?' inquired I.

'It is the wolf that devoured Little Red Riding Hood,' answered the Virtuoso; 'and by his side—with a milder and more matronly look, as you perceive—stands the she-wolf that suckled Romulus and Remus.'

'Ah, indeed!' exclaimed I. 'And what lovely lamb is this with the snow-white fleece, which seems to be of as delicate a texture as innocence itself?'

'Methinks you have but carelessly read Spenser,' replied my guide, 'or you would at once recognise the " milk-white lamb " which

Una led. But I set no great value upon the lamb. The next specimen is better worth our notice.'

'What!' cried I, 'this strange animal with the black head of an ox upon the body of a white horse? Were it possible to suppose it, I should say that this was Alexander's steed, Bucephalus.'

'The same,' said the Virtuoso. 'And can you likewise give a name to the famous charger that stands beside him?'

Next to the renewed Bucephalus stood the mere skeleton of a horse, with the white bones peeping through his ill-conditioned hide; but, if my heart had not warmed towards that pitiful anatomy, I might as well have quitted the museum at once. Its rarities had not been collected with pain and toil from the four quarters of the earth, and from the depths of the sea, and from the palaces and sepulchres of ages, for those who could mistake this illustrious steed.

'It is Rosinante!' exclaimed I, with enthusiasm.

And so it proved. My admiration for the noble and gallant horse caused me to glance with less interest at the other animals, although many of them might have deserved the notice of Cuvier himself. There was the donkey which Peter Bell cudgelled so soundly, and a brother of the same species who had suffered a similar infliction from the ancient prophet Balaam. Some doubts were entertained, however, as to the authenticity of the latter beast. My guide pointed out the venerable Argus, the faithful dog of Ulysses, and also another dog (for so the skin bespoke it), which, though imperfectly preserved, seemed once to have had three heads. It was Cerberus. I was considerably amused at detecting in an obscure corner the fox that became so famous by the loss of his tail. There were several stuffed cats, which, as a dear lover of that comfortable beast, attracted my affectionate regards. One was Dr. Johnson's cat Hodge ; and in the same row stood the favourite cats of Mahomet, Gray, and Sir Walter Scott, together with Puss in Boots,

and a cat of very noble aspect who had once
been a deity of ancient Egypt. Byron's
tame bear came next. I must not forget to
mention the Erymanthean boar, the skin of
St. George's Dragon, and that of the serpent
Python ; and another skin with beautifully
variegated hues, supposed to have been the
garment of the 'spirited sly snake' which
tempted Eve. Against the walls were suspended the horn of the stag that Shakspeare
shot ; and on the floor lay the ponderous
shell of the tortoise which fell upon the head
of Æschylus. In one row, as natural as life,
stood the sacred bull Apis, the cow 'with
the crumpled horn,' and a very wild-looking
young heifer, which I guessed to be the cow
that jumped over the moon. She was
probably killed by the rapidity of her descent.
As I turned away, my eyes fell upon an
indescribable monster, which proved to be a
griffin.

'I look in vain,' observed I, 'for the skin
of an animal which might well deserve the

closest study of a naturalist—the winged horse, Pegasus.'

' He is not yet dead,' replied the Virtuoso ; ' but he is so hard ridden by many young gentlemen of the day, that I hope soon to add his skin and skeleton to my collection.'

We now passed to the next alcove of the hall, in which was a multitude of stuffed birds. They were very prettily arranged, some upon the branches of trees, others brooding upon nests, and others suspended by wires so artificially, that they seemed to be in the very act of flight. Among them was a white dove, with a withered branch of olive-leaves in her mouth.

' Can this be the very dove ?' enquired I, ' that brought the message of peace and hope to the tempest-beaten passengers of the ark ?'

' Even so,' said my companion.

' And this raven, I suppose,' continued I, ' is the same that fed Elijah in the wilderness.'

' The raven ? No,' said the Virtuoso ; ' it

is a bird of modern date. He belonged to one Barnaby Rudge; and many people fancied that the devil himself was disguised under his sable plumage. But poor Grip has drawn his last cork, and has been forced to "say die" at last. This other raven, harldly less curious, is that in which the soul of King George I. revisited his lady-love, the Duchess of Kendall.

My guide next pointed out Minerva's owl and the vulture that preyed upon the liver of Prometheus. There was, likewise, the sacred Ibis of Egypt, and one of the Stymphalides which Hercules shot in his sixth labour. Shelley's skylark, Bryant's water-fowl, and a pigeon from the belfry of the Old South Church, preserved by N. P. Willis, were placed on the same perch. I could not but shudder on beholding Coleridge's albatross, transfixed with the ancient mariner's crossbow shaft. Beside this bird of awful poesy stood a grey goose of very ordinary aspect.

' Stuffed goose is no such rarity,' observed

I. 'Why do you preserve such a specimen in your museum ?'

'It is one of the flock whose cackling saved the Roman Capitol,' answered the Virtuoso. 'Many geese have cackled and hissed both before and since ; but none, like these, have clamoured themselves into immortality.'

There seemed to be little else that demanded notice in this department of the museum, unless we except Robinson Crusoe's parrot, a live phœnix, a footless bird of paradise, and a splendid peacock, supposed to be the same that once contained the soul of Pythagoras. I therefore passed to the next alcove, the shelves of which were covered with a miscellaneous collection of curiosities such as are usually found in similar establishments. One of the first things that took my eye was a strange-looking cap, woven of some substance that appeared to be neither woollen, cotton, nor linen.

'Is this a magician's cap ?' I asked.

'No,' replied the Virtuoso ; 'it is merely

Dr. Franklin's cap of asbesta. But here is one which, perhaps, may suit you better. It is the wishing cap of Fortunatus. Will you try it on ?'

' By no means,' answered I, putting it aside with my hand. ' The day of wild wishes is past with me. I desire nothing that may not come in the ordinary course of Providence.'

' Then, probably,' returned the Virtuoso ; ' you will not be tempted to rub this lamp ?'

While speaking, he took from the shelf an antique brass lamp, curiously wrought with embossed figures, but so covered with verdigris that the sculpture was almost eaten away.

' It is a thousand years,' said he, ' since the genius of this lamp constructed Aladdin's palace in a single night. But he still retains his power ; and the man who rubs Aladdin's lamp has but to desire either a palace or a cottage.'

' I might desire a cottage,' replied I ; ' but I would have it founded on sure and stable truth, not on dreams and phantasies. I have learned to look for the real and true.'

My guide next showed me Prospero's magic wand, broken into three fragments by the hand of its mighty master. On the same shelf lay the gold ring of ancient Gyges, which enabled the wearer to walk invisible. On the other side of the alcove was a tall looking-glass in a frame of ebony, but veiled with a curtain of purple silk, through the rents of which the gleam of the mirror was perceptible.

'This is Cornelius Agrippa's magic glass,' observed the Virtuoso. 'Draw aside the curtain, and picture any human form within your mind, and it will be reflected in the mirror.'

'It is enough if I can picture it within my mind,' answered I. 'Why should I wish it to be repeated in the mirror? But, indeed, these works of magic have grown wearisome to me. There are so many greater wonders in the world, to those who keep their eyes open and their sight undimmed by custom, that all the delusions of the old sorcerers seem flat and stale. Unless you can show me something really curious, I care not to look further into your museum.'

'Ah, well then,' said the Virtuoso, composedly, 'perhaps you may deem some of my antiquarian rarities deserving of a glance.'

He pointed out the iron mask, now corroded with rust; and my heart grew sick at the sight of this dreadful relic, which had shut out a human being from sympathy with his race. There was nothing half so terrible in the axe that beheaded King Charles, nor in the dagger that slew Henry of Navarre, nor in the arrow that pierced the heart of William Rufus—all of which were shown to me. Many of the articles derived their interest, such as it was, from having been formerly in the possession of royalty. For instance, here was Charlemagne's sheepskin cloak, the flowing wig of Louis Quatorze, the spinning-wheel of Sardanapalus, and King Stephen's famous breeches which cost him but a crown.

The heart of the Bloody Mary, with the word 'Calais' worn into its diseased substance, was preserved in a bottle of spirits; and near it lay the golden case in which the queen of Gustavus Adolphus treasured up that hero's heart. Among these relics and heirlooms of kings, I must not forget the long, hairy ears of Midas, and a piece of bread which had been changed to gold by the touch of that unlucky monarch. And as Grecian Helen was a queen, it may here be mentioned that I was permitted to take into my hand a lock of her golden hair and the bowl which a sculptor modelled from the curve of her perfect breast. Here, likewise, was the robe that smothered Agamemnon, Nero's fiddle, the Czar Peter's brandy-bottle, the crown of Semiramis, and Canute's sceptre which he extended over the sea. That my own land may not deem itself neglected, let me add that I was favoured with a sight of the skull of King Philip, the famous Indian chief, whose head the Puritans smote off, and exhibited upon a pole.

'Show me something else,' said I to the Virtuoso. 'Kings are in such an artificial position that people in the ordinary walks of life cannot feel an interest in their relics. If you could show me the straw hat of sweet little Nell, I would far rather see it than a king's golden crown.'

'There it is,' said my guide, pointing carelessly with his staff to the straw hat in question. 'But, indeed, you are hard to please. Here are the seven-league boots. Will you try them on?'

'Our modern railroads have superseded their use,' answered I ; 'and as to these cowhide boots, I could show you quite as curious a pair at the Transcendental Community in Roxbury.'

We next examined a collection of swords and other weapons, belonging to different epochs, but thrown together without much attempt at arrangement. Here was Arthur's sword Excalibur, and that of the Cid Campeador, and the sword of Brutus rusted with Cæsar's blood and his own, and the sword of

Joan of Arc, and that of Horatius, and that with which Virginius slew his daughter, and the one which Dionysius suspended over the head of Damocles. Here, also, was Arria's sword, which she plunged into her own breast, in order to taste of death before her husband. The crooked blade of Saladin's scimitar next attracted my notice. I know not by what chance, but so it happened, that the sword of one of our own militia generals was suspended between Don Quixote's lance and the brown blade of Hudibras. My heart throbbed high at the sight of the helmet of Miltiades, and the spear that was broken in the breast of Epaminondas. I recognised the shield of Achilles by its resemblance to the admirable cast in the possession of Professor Felton. Nothing in this apartment interested me more than Major Pitcairn's pistol, the discharge of which, at Lexington, began the war of revolution, and was reverberated in thunder around the land for seven long years. The bow of Ulysses, though unstrung for ages, was placed against the wall, together with a sheaf of Robin Hood's arrows and the rifle of Daniel Boone.

'Enough of weapons,' said I, at length; 'although I would gladly have seen the sacred shield which fell from heaven in the time of Numa. And surely you should obtain the sword which Washington un- sheathed at Cambridge. But the collection does you much credit. Let us pass on.'

In the next alcove we saw the golden thigh of Pythagoras which had so divine a meaning ; and, by one of the queer analogies to which the Virtuoso seemed to be addicted, this ancient emblem lay on the same shelf with Peter Stuyvesaut's wooden leg, that was fabled to be of silver. Here was a remnant of the Golden Fleece, and a sprig of yellow leaves that resembled the foliage of a frost- bitten elm, but was duly authenticated as a portion of the golden branch by which Æneas gained admittance to the realms of Pluto. Atalanta's golden apple, and one of the apples of discord, were wrapped in the napkin of gold which Rampsinitus brought from Hades ; and the whole were deposited in the golden vase of Bias, with its inscription, ' To the Wisest.'

' And how did you obtain this vase ? ' said I to the Virtuoso.

'It was given me long ago,' replied he, with a scornful expression in his eye, ' because I had learned to despise all things.'

It had not escaped me that, though the Virtuoso was evidently a man of high cultivation, yet he seemed to lack sympathy with the spiritual, the sublime, and the tender. Apart from the whim that had led him to devote so much time, pains, and expense, to the collection of this museum, he impressed me as one of the hardest and coldest men of the world whom I had ever met.

' To despise all things!' repeated I. ' This, at best, is the wisdom of the understanding. It is the creed of a man whose soul, whose better and diviner part, has never been awakened, or has died out of him.'

'I did not think that you were still so young,' said the Virtuoso. 'Should you live to my years you will acknowledge that the vase of Bias was not ill-bestowed.'

Without further discussion of the point he directed my attention to other curiosities. I examined Cinderella's little glass slipper, and compared it with one of Diana's sandals, and with Fanny Elssler's shoe, which bore testimony to the muscular character of her illustrious foot. On the same shelf were Thomas the Rhymer's green velvet shoes, and the brazen shoe of Empedocles which was thrown out of Mount Etna. Anacreon's drinking-cup was placed in apt juxtaposition with one of Tom Moore's wine glasses and Circe's magic bowl. There were symbols of luxury and riot; but near them stood the cup whence Socrates drank his hemlock, and that which Sir Philip Sydney put from his death-parched lips to bestow the draught upon a dying soldier. Next appeared a cluster of tobacco-pipes, consisting of Sir Walter Raleigh's (the earliest on record), Dr.

Parr's, Charles Lamb's, and the first calumet of peace which was ever smoked between a European and an Indian. Among other musical instruments, I noticed the lyre of Orpheus, and those of Homer and Sappho, Dr. Franklin's famous whistle, the trumpet of Anthony van Corlear, and the flute which Goldsmith played upon in his rambles through the French provinces. The staff of Peter the Hermit stood in a corner with that of good old Bishop Jewel, and one of ivory, which had belonged to Papirius, the Roman senator. The ponderous club of Hercules was close at hand. The Virtuoso showed me the chisel of Phidias, Claude's palette, and the brush of Apelles, observing that he intended to bestow the former either on Greenough, Crawford, or Powers, and the two latter upon Washington Allston. There was a small vase of oracular gas from Delphos, which I trust will be submitted to the scientific analysis of Professor Silliman. I was deeply moved on beholding a vial of the tears into which Niobe was dissolved, nor less so on learning that a shapeless fragment of salt was a relic of that victim of despondency and sinful regrets—Lot's wife. My companion appeared to set great value upon some Egyptian darkness in a blacking jug. Several of the shelves were covered by a collection of coins, among which, however, I remember none but the Splendid Shilling, celebrated by Phillips, and a dollar's worth of the iron money of Lycurgus, weighing about fifty pounds.

Walking carelessly onward I had nearly fallen over a huge bundle, like a pedlar's pack, done up in sackcloth, and very securely strapped and corded.

'It is Christian's burden of sin,' said the Virtuoso.

'O pray let us open it!' cried I. 'For many a year I have longed to know its contents.'

'Look into your own consciousness and memory,' replied the Virtuoso. 'You will there find a list of whatever it contains.'

As this was an undeniable truth, I threw

a melancholy look at the burden and passed on. A collection of old garments, hanging on pegs, was worthy of some attention, especially the shirt of Nessus, Cæsar's mantle, Joseph's coat of many colours, the Vicar of Bray's cassock, Goldsmith's peach-bloom suit, a pair of President Jefferson's scarlet breeches, John Randolph's red baize hunting shirt, the drab small clothes of the Stout Gentleman, and the rags of the 'man all tattered and torn.' George Fox's hat impressed me with deep reverence as a relic of perhaps the truest apostle that has appeared on earth for these eighteen hundred years. My eye was next attracted by an old pair of shears, which I should have taken for the memorial of some famous tailor, only that the Virtuoso pledged his veracity that they were the identical scissors of Atropos. He also showed me a broken hour-glass which had been thrown aside by Father Time, together with the old gentleman's grey fore-lock tastefully braided into a brooch. In the hour-glass was the handful of sand, the grains of which had numbered the years of the Cumœan Sibyl. I think it was in this alcove that I saw the inkstand which Luther threw at the devil, and the ring which Essex, while under sentence of death, sent to Queen Elizabeth. And here was the blood-incrusted pen of steel with which Faust signed away his salvation.

The Virtuoso now opened the door of a closet and showed me a lamp burning, while three others stood unlighted by its side. One of the three was the lamp of Diogenes, another that of Guy Fawkes, and the third that which Hero set forth to the midnight breeze in the high tower of Abydos.

'See!' said the Virtuoso, blowing with all his force at the lighted lamp.

The flame quivered and shrank away from his breath, but clung to the wick, and resumed its brilliancy as soon as the blast was exhausted.

'It is an undying lamp from the tomb of Charlemagne,' observed my guide. 'That flame was kindled a thousand years ago.

'How ridiculous to kindle an unnatural light in tombs!' exclaimed I. 'We should seek to behold the dead in the light of heaven. But what is the meaning of this chafing-dish of glowing coals?'

'That,' answered the Virtuoso, 'is the original fire which Prometheus stole from heaven. Look stedfastly into it, and you will discern another curiosity.'

I gazed into that fire—which, symbolically, was the origin of all that was bright and glorious in the soul of man,— and in the midst of it, behold, a little reptile sporting with evident enjoyment of the fervid heat! It was a Salamander.

'What a sacrilege,' cried I, with inexpressible disgust. 'Can you find no better use for this ethereal fire than to cherish a loathsome reptile in it? Yet there are men who abuse the sacred fire of their own souls to as foul and guilty a purpose.'

The Virtuoso made no answer except by a dry laugh, and an assurance that the Salamander was the very same which Benvenuto

Cellini had seen in his father's household fire. He then proceeded to show me other rarities; for this closet appeared to be the receptacle of what he considered most valuable in his collection.

'There,' said he, 'is the Great Carbuncle of the White Mountains.'

I gazed with no little interest at this mighty gem, which it had been one of the wild projects of my youth to discover. Possibly it might have looked brighter to me in those days than now; at all events, it had not such brilliancy as to detain me long from the other articles of the Museum. The Virtuoso pointed out to me a crystalline stone, which hung by a gold chain against the wall.

'That is the philosopher's stone,' said he.

'And have you the elixir vitæ, which generally accompanies it?' enquired I.

'Even so; this urn is filled with it,' he replied. 'A draught would refresh you. Here is Hebe's cup; will you quaff a health from it?'

My heart thrilled within me at the idea of such a reviving draught; for methought I had great need of it after travelling so far on the dusty road of life. But I know not whether it were a peculiar glance in the Virtuoso's eye, or the circumstance that this most precious liquid was contained in an antique sepulchre urn, that made me pause. Then came many a thought with which, in the calmer and better hours of life, I had strengthened myself to feel that Death is the very friend whom, in his due season, even the happiest mortal should be willing to embrace.

'No; I desire no earthly immortality,' said I. 'Were man to live longer on the earth, the spiritual would die out of him. The spark of ethereal fire would be choked by the material, the sensual. There is a celestial something within us that requires, after a certain time, the atmosphere of heaven to preserve it from decay and ruin. I will have none of this liquid. You do well to keep it in a sepulchral urn; for it would produce death while bestowing the shadow of life.'

'All this is unintelligible to me,' responded the guide, with indifference. 'Life—earthly life—is the only good. But you refuse the draught. Well, it is not likely to be offered twice within one man's experience. Probably you have griefs which you seek to forget in death. I can enable you to forget them in life. Will you take a draught of Lethe?'

As he spoke the Virtuoso took from the shelf a crystal vase containing a sable liquor, which caught no reflected image from the objects around.

'Not for the world!' exclaimed I, shrinking back. 'I can spare none of my recollections, not even those of error or sorrow. They are all alike the food of my spirit. As well never to have lived as to lose them now.'

Without further parley we passed to the next alcove, the shelves of which were burdened with ancient volumes, and with those

rolls of papyrus in which was treasured up the
eldest wisdom of the earth. Perhaps the most
valuable work in the collection, to a biblioma-
niac, was the Book of Hermes. For my part,
however, I would have given a higher price for
those six of the Sibyl's books which Tarquin
refused to purchase, and which the Virtuoso
informed me he had himself found in the
cave of Trophonius.   Doubtless these old
volumes contain prophecies of the fate of
Rome, both as respects the decline and fall
of her temporal empire, and the rise of her
spiritual one.   Not without value, likewise,
was the work of Anaxagoras on Nature,
hitherto supposed to be irrecoverably lost,
and the missing treatises of Longinus, by
which modern criticism might profit, and
these books of Livy for which the classic
student has so long sorrowed without hope.
Among these precious tomes I observed the
original manuscript of the Koran, and also
that of the Mormon Bible in Joe Smith's
authentic autograph. Alexander's copy of
the Iliad was also there, enclosed in the

jewelled casket of Darius, still fragrant of the perfumes which the Persian kept in it.

Opening an iron clasped volume, bound in black leather, I discovered it to be Cornelius Agrippa's book of magic ; and it was rendered still more interesting by the fact that many flowers, ancient and modern, were pressed between its leaves. Here was a rose from Eve's bridal bower ; and all those red and white roses which were plucked in the garden of the Temple by the partisans of York and Lancaster. Here was Halleck's wild rose of Alloway. Cowper had contributed a sensitive plant, and Wordsworth an eglantine, and Burns a mountain daisy, and Kirke White a star of Bethlehem, and Longfellow a spray of fennel, with its yellow flowers. James Russell Lowell had given a Pressed Flower, but fragrant still, which had been shadowed in the Rhine. There was also a sprig from Southey's Holly Tree. One of the most beautiful specimens was a fringed gentian, which had been plucked and preserved for immortality by Bryant. From

Jones Very, a poet whose voice is scarce heard among us by reason of its depth, there was a Wind Flower, and a Columbine.

As I closed Cornelius Agrippa's magic volume, an old, mildewed letter fell upon the floor. It proved to be an autograph from the Flying Dutchman to his wife. I could linger no longer among books; for the after noon was waning, and there was yet much to see. The bare mention of a few more curiosities must suffice. The immense skull of Polyphemus was recognisable by the cavernous hollow in the centre of the fore-head where once had blazed the giant's single eye. The tub of Diogenes, Medea's caldron, and Psyche's vase of beauty were placed one within another. Pandora's box, without the lid, stood next, containing nothing but the girdle of Venus, which had been carelessly flung into it. A bundle of birch rods, which had been used by Shen-stone's schoolmistress, were tied up with the Countess of Salisbury's garter. I knew not which to value most, a roc's egg, as big as an ordinary hog's head, or the shell of the egg which Columbus set upon its end. Perhaps the most delicate article in the whole museum was Queen Mab's chariot, which, to guard it from the touch of meddlesome fingers, was placed under a glass tumbler.

Several of the shelves were occupied by specimens of entomology. Feeling but little interest in the science, I noticed only Anacreon's grasshopper, and a humble bee which had been presented to the Virtuoso by Ralph Waldo Emerson.

In the part of the hall which we had now reached I observed a curtain, that descended from the ceiling to the floor in voluminous folds, of a depth, richness, and magnificence which I have never seen equalled. It was not to be doubted that this splendid though dark and solemn veil concealed a portion of the museum even richer in wonders than that through which I had already passed ; but, on my attempting to grasp the edge of the curtain and draw it aside, it proved to be an illusive picture.

'You need not blush,' remarked the Virtuoso; 'for that same curtain deceived Zeuxis. It is the celebrated painting of Parrhasius.'

In a range with the curtain there were a number of other choice pictures by artists of ancient days. Here was the famous cluster of grapes by Zeuxis, so admirably depicted that it seemed as if the ripe juice were bursting forth. As to the picture of the old woman by the same illustrious painter, which was so ludicrous that he himself died with laughing at it, I cannot say that it particularly moved my risibility. Ancient humour seems to have little power over modern muscles. Here, also, was the horse painted by Apelles which living horses neighed at; his first portrait of Alexander the Great, and his last unfinished picture of Venus asleep. Each of these works of art, together with others by Parrhasius, Timanthes, Polygnotus, Apollodorus, Pausias, and Pamphilus required more time to study than I could bestow for the adequate perception of their merits. I shall therefore leave them undescribed and uncriticised, nor attempt to settle the question of superiority between ancient and modern art.

For the same reason I shall pass lightly over the specimens of antique sculpture which this indefatigable and fortunate Virtuoso had dug out of the dust of fallen empires. Here was Ætoin's cedar statue of Æsculapius, much decayed, and Alcon's iron statue of Hercules, lamentably rusted. Here was the statue of Victory, six feet high, which the Jupiter Olympus of Phydias had held in his hand. Here was a forefinger of the Colossus of Rhodes, seven feet in length. Here was a Venus Urania of Phidias, and other images of male and female beauty or grandeur, wrought by sculptors who appeared never to have debased their souls by the sight of any meaner forms than those of gods or godlike mortals. But the deep simplicity of these great works was not to be comprehended by a mind excited and disturbed, as mine was, by the various objects that had recently been presented to it. I therefore turned away with merely a passing glance, resolving on some future occasion to brood over each individual statue and picture until my inmost spirit should feel their excellence. In this department, again, I noticed the tendency to whimsical combinations and ludicrous analogies which seemed to influence many of the arrangements of the museum. The wooden statue so well known as the Palladium of Troy was placed in close apposition with the wooden head of General Jackson, which was stolen a few years since from the bows of the frigate 'Constitution.'

We had now completed the circuit of the spacious hall, and found ourselves again near the door. Feeling somewhat wearied with the survey of so many novelties and antiquities, I sat down upon Cowper's sofa, while the Virtuoso threw himself carelessly into Rabelais' easy chair. Casting my eyes upon the opposite wall, I was surprised to perceive the shadow of a man flickering unsteadily across the wainscot, and looking as if it were stirred by some breath of air that found its way through the door or window. No substantial figure was visible from which this shadow might be thrown ; nor, had there been such, was there any sunshine that would have caused it to darken upon the wall.

' It is Peter Schlemihl's shadow,' observed the Virtuoso, ' and one of the most valuable articles in my collection.'

' Methinks a shadow would have made a fitting doorkeeper to such a museum,' said I ; ' although, indeed, yonder figure has something strange and fantastic about him, which suits well enough with many of the impressions which I have received here. Pray, who is he ?'

While speaking, I gazed more scrutinizingly than before at the antiquated presence of the person who had admitted me, and who still sat on his bench with the same restless aspect and dim, confused, questioning anxiety that I had noticed on his first entrance. At this moment he looked eagerly towards us, and, half starting from his seat, addressed me.

'I beseech you, kind sir,' said he, in a cracked, melancholy tone, 'have pity on the most unfortunate man in the world. For heaven's sake, answer me a single question! Is this the town of Boston?'

'You have recognised him now,' said the Virtuoso. 'It is Peter Rigg, the missing man. I chanced to meet him the other day still in search of Boston, and conducted him hither; and, as he could not succeed in finding his friends, I have taken him into my service as doorkeeper. He is somewhat apt to ramble, but otherwise a man of trust and integrity.'

'And might I venture to ask,' continued I, 'to whom I am indebted for this afternoon's gratification?'

The Virtuoso, before replying, laid his hand upon an antique dart, or javelin, the rusty steel head of which seemed to have been blunted, as if it had encountered the resistance of a tempered shield, or breastplate.

'My name has not been without its distinction in the world for a longer period than that of any other man alive,' answered he.

'Yet many doubt my existence ; perhaps you will do so to-morrow. This dart which I hold in my hand was once grim Death's weapon. I served him well for the space of four thousand years ; but it fell blunted, as you see, when he directed it against my breast.'

These words were spoken with the calm and cold courtesy of manner that had characterised this singular personage throughout our interview. I fancied, it is true, that there was a bitterness indefinably mingled with his tone, as of one cut off from natural sympathies, and blasted with a doom that had been inflicted on no other human being, and by the results of which he had ceased to be human. Yet, withal, it seemed one of the most terrible consequences of that doom that the victim no longer regarded it as a calamity, but had finally accepted it as the greatest good that could have befallen him.

'You are the Wandering Jew?' exclaimed I.

The Virtuoso bowed without emotion of any kind ; for, by centuries of custom, he had almost lost the sense of strangeness in his fate, and was but imperfectly conscious of the astonishment and awe with which it affected such as are capable of death.

'Your doom is indeed a fearful one!' said I, with irrepressible feeling and a frankness that afterwards startled me; 'yet perhaps the ethereal spirit is not entirely extinct under all this corrupted or frozen mass of earthly life. Perhaps the immortal spark may yet be re-kindled by a breath of heaven. Perhaps you may yet be permitted to die before it is too late to live eternally. You have my prayers for such a consummation. Farewell!'

'Your prayers will be vain,' replied he, with a smile of cold triumph. 'My destiny is linked with the realities of earth. You are welcome to your visions and shadows of a future state; but give me what I can see, and touch, and understand, and I ask no more.'

'It is indeed too late,' thought I. 'The soul is dead within him.'

Struggling between pity and horror, I ex-tended my hand, to which the Virtuoso gave his own, still with the habitual courtesy of a man of the world, but without a single throb of human brotherhood. The touch seemed like ice, yet I know not whether morally or physically. As I departed, he bade me observe that the inner door of the hall was constructed with the ivory leaves of the gateway through which Æneas and the Sibyl had been dismissed from Hades.

PICTURE to yourselves a handsome old-fashioned room, with a large, open cupboard at one end, in which is displayed a magnificent gold cup, with some other splendid articles of gold and silver plate. In another part of the room, opposite to a tall looking-glass, sits a man of strong and sturdy frame, whose face has been roughened by northern tempests, and blackened by the burning sun of the West Indies. He wears an immense periwig, flowing down over his shoulders. His coat has a wide embroidery of golden foliage ; and his waistcoast, likewise, is all flowered over and bedizened with gold. His red, rough hands, which have done many a good day's work with hammer and adze, are half-covered by the delicate lace ruffles at his wrists. On a table lies his silver-hilted sword ; and in a corner of the room stands his gold-headed cane, made of a beautifully polished West India wood.

Somewhat such an aspect as this did Sir William Phipps present when he sat in his chair, after the King had appointed him Governor of Massachusetts. But Sir William Phipps had not always worn a gold embroidered coat, nor always sat so much at his ease. He was a poor man's son, and was born in the province of Maine, where he used to tend sheep upon the hills in his boyhood and youth. Until he had grown to be a man he did not even know how to read and write. Tired of tending sheep, he next apprenticed himself to a ship carpenter, and spent about four years in hewing the crooked limbs of oak-trees into knees for vessels.

In 1673, when he was twenty-two years old, he came to Boston, and soon afterwards was married to a widow-lady, who had property enough to set him up in business. It was not long, however, before he lost all the money that he had acquired by his marriage and became a poor man again. Still he was not discouraged. He often told his wife that, some time or other, he should be very rich, and would build a 'fair brick house' in the Green Lane of Boston.

You must not suppose that he had been to a fortune-teller to enquire his destiny. It was his own energy and spirit of enterprise, and his resolution to lead an industrious life, that made him look forward with so much confidence to better days.

Several years passed away, and William Phipps had not yet gained the riches which he promised to himself. During this time he had begun to follow the sea for a living. In the year 1684 he happened to hear of a Spanish ship which had been cast away near the Bahama Islands, and which was supposed to contain a great deal of gold and silver. Phipps went to the place in a small vessel, hoping that he should be able to recover some of the treasure from the wreck. He did not succeed, however, in fishing up gold and silver enough to pay the expenses of his voyage.

But before he returned he was told of another Spanish ship, or galleon, which had been cast away near Porto de la Plata. She had now lain as much as fifty years beneath the waves. This old ship had been ladened with immense wealth ; and hitherto nobody had thought of the possibility of recovering any part of it from the deep sea which was rolling and tossing it about. But though it was now an old story, and the most aged people had almost forgotten that such a vessel had been wrecked, William Phipps resolved that the sunken treasure should again be brought to light.

He went to London and obtained admittance to King James, who had not yet been driven from his throne. He told the king of the vast wealth that was lying at the bottom of the sea. King James listened with attention, and thought this a fine opportunity to fill his treasury with Spanish gold. He appointed William Phipps to be captain of a vessel, called the ' Rose Algier,' carrying eighteen guns and ninety-five men. So now he was Captain Phipps of the English navy.

Captain Phipps sailed from England in the ' Rose Algier,' and cruised for nearly two years in the West Indies, endeavouring to find the wreck of the Spanish ship. But the sea is so wide and deep, that it is no easy matter to discover the exact spot where a sunken vessel lies. The prospect of success seemed very small ; and most people would have thought that Captain Phipps was as far from having money enough to build a ' fair brick house,' as he was while he tended sheep.

The seamen of the ' Rose Algier ' became discouraged, and gave up all hopes of making their fortunes by discovering the Spanish wreck. They wanted to compel Captain Phipps to turn pirate. There was a much better prospect, they thought, of growing rich by plundering vessels which still sailed in the sea, than by seeking for a ship which had lain beneath the waves for half a century.

They broke out in open mutiny; but were finally mastered by Phipps, and compelled to obey his orders. It would have been dangerous, however, to continue much longer at sea with such a crew of mutinous sailors; and besides the 'Rose Algier' was leaky and unseaworthy. So Captain Phipps judged it best to return to England.

Before leaving the West Indies he met with a Spaniard, an old man, who remembered the wreck of the Spanish ship, and gave him directions how to find the very spot. It was on a reef of rocks, a few leagues from Porto de la Plata.

On his arrival in England, therefore, Captain Phipps solicited the king to let him have another vessel and send him back again to the West Indies. But King James, who had probably expected that the 'Rose Algier' would return laden with gold, refused to have anything more to do with the affair. Phipps might never have been able to renew the search if the Duke of Albemarle and some other nobleman had not lent their assistance. They fitted out a ship, and gave the command to Captain Phipps. He sailed from England, and arrived safely at Porto de la Plata, where he took an adze, and assisted his men to build a large boat.

The boat was intended for the purpose of going closer to the reef of rocks than a large vessel could safely venture. When it was finished, the captain sent several men in it to examine the spot where the Spanish ship was said to have been wrecked. They were accompanied by some Indians, who were skilful divers, and could go down a great way into the depths of the sea.

The boat's crew proceeded to the reef of rocks, and rowed round and round it a great many times. They gazed down into the water, which was so transparent that it seemed as if they could have seen the gold and silver at the bottom, had there been any of those precious metals there. Nothing, however, could they see; nothing more valuable than a curious sea-shrub, which was growing beneath the water, in a crevice of the reef of rocks. It flaunted to and fro with the swell and reflux of the waves, and looked as if its leaves were gold.

'We won't go back empty-handed,' cried an English sailor; and then he spoke to one of the Indian divers. 'Dive down and bring me that pretty sea-shrub there. That's the only treasure we shall find.'

Down plunged the diver, and soon rose dripping from the water, holding the sea-shrub in his hand. But he had learned some news at the bottom of the sea.

'There are some ship's guns,' said he, the moment he had drawn breath, 'some great cannon among the rocks, near where the shrub was growing.'

No sooner had he spoken than the English sailors knew that they had found the very spot where the Spanish galleon had been wrecked so many years before. The other Indian divers immediately plunged over the boat's side and swam headlong down, groping among the rocks and sunken cannon. In a few moments one of them rose above the water with a heavy lump of silver in his arms. The single lump was worth more than a thousand dollars. The sailors took it into the boat, and then rowed back as speedily as they could, being in haste to inform Captain Phipps of their good luck.

But, confidently as the captain had hoped to find the Spanish wreck, yet, now that it was really found, the news seemed too good to be true. He could not believe it till the sailors showed him the lump of silver.

'Thanks be to God!' then cries Captain Phipps. 'We shall every man of us make our fortunes.'

Hereupon the captain and all the crew set to work with iron rakes, and great hooks and lines, fishing for gold and silver at the bottom of the sea. Up came the treasure in abundance. Now they beheld a table of solid silver, once the property of an old Spanish grandee. Now they found a sacramental vessel which had been destined as a gift to some Catholic church. Now they drew up a golden cup, fit for the King of

Spain to drink his wine out of. Perhaps the bony hand of its former owner had been grasping the precious cup, and was drawn up along with it. Now their rakes or fishing-lines were loaded with masses of silver bullion. There were also precious stones among the treasure, glittering and sparkling, so that it is a wonder their radiance could have been concealed.

There is something sad and terrible in the idea of snatching all this wealth from the devouring ocean, which had possessed it for such a length of years. It seems as if men had no right to make themselves rich with it. It ought to have been left with the skeletons of the ancient Spaniards, who had been drowned when the ship was wrecked, and whose bones were scattered among the gold and silver.

But Captain Phipps and his crew were troubled with no such thoughts as these. After a day or two they lighted on another part of the wreck, where they found a great many bags of silver dollars. But nobody could have guessed that these were money-bags. By remaining so long in the salt-water they had become covered over with a crust which had the appearance of stone, so that it was necessary to break them in pieces with hammers and axes. When this was done, a stream of silver dollars gushed out upon the deck of the vessel.

The whole value of the recovered treasure, plate, bullion, precious stones, and all, was estimated at more than two millions of dollars. It was dangerous even to look at such a vast amount of wealth. A sea-captain, who had assisted Phipps in the enterprise, utterly lost his reason at the sight of it. He died two years afterwards, still raving about the treasures that lie at the bottom of the sea. It would have been better for this man if he had left the skeletons of the shipwrecked Spaniards in quiet possession of their wealth.

Captain Phipps and his men continued to fish up plate, bullion, and dollars as plentifully as ever, till their provisions grew short.

Then, as they could not feed upon gold and silver any more than old King Midas could, they found it necessary to go in quest of better sustenance. Phipps resolved to return to England. He arrived there in 1687, and was received with great joy by the Duke of Albemarle and other English lords who had fitted out the vessel. Well they might rejoice ; for they took by far the greater part of the treasure to themselves.

The captain's share, however, was enough to make him comfortable for the rest of his days. It also enabled him to fulfil his promise to his wife by building a ' fair brick house ' in the Green Lane of Boston. The Duke of Albemarle sent Mrs. Phipps a magnificent gold cup worth at least five thousand dollars. Before Captain Phipps left London, King James made him a knight ; so that, instead of the obscure ship-carpenter who had formerly dwelt among them, the inhabitants of Boston welcomed him on his return as the rich and famous Sir William Phipps.

But Sir William Phipps was too active and adventurous a man to sit still in the quiet enjoyment of his good fortune. In the year 1690 he went on a military expedition against the French colonies in America, conquered the whole province of Acadia, and returned to Boston with a great deal of plunder. In the same year he took command of an expedition against Quebec, but did not succeed in capturing that city. In 1692, being then in London, King William III. appointed him Governor of Massachusetts. Within the limits of this province were now included the old colony of Plymouth, and the territories of Maine and Nova Scotia. Sir William Phipps had likewise brought with him a new charter from the king, which served instead of a constitution, and set forth the method in which the province was to be governed. Under the first charter the people had been the source of all power. Winthrop, Endicott, Bradstreet, and the rest of them, had been governors by the choice of the people, with-

out any interference of the king.   But hence-
forth the governor was to hold his station
solely by the king's appointment and during
his pleasure ; and the same was the case
with the lieutenant-governor, and some other
high officers.   The people, however, were
still allowed to choose representatives, and
the governor's council was chosen by the
general court.

It is highly probable, however, that even
had the election still remained with the
people, Sir William Phipps would have been
a successful candidate : for his adventures
and military exploits had gained him a sort
of renown, which always goes a great way
with the people.   And he had many popular
characteristics, being a kind, warm-hearted
man, not ashamed of his low origin, nor
haughty in his present elevation.   Soon after
his arrival he proved that he did not blush
to recognise his former associates.

He made a grand festival at his new brick
house, and invited all the ship-carpenters of
Boston to be his guests.   At the head of the

table sat Sir William Phipps himself, treating these hard-handed men as his brethren, cracking jokes with them, and talking familiarly about old times.

As a governor, however, there was great fault found with him by-and-bye. Very soon after he had assumed the government, he became engaged in a very frightful business which might have perplexed a wiser and better cultivated head than his. This was the witchcraft delusion—a frenzy which led to the death of many innocent persons, and had originated in the wicked arts of a few children. They belonged to the Rev. Mr. Parris, minister of Salem. These children complained of being pinched and pricked with pins, and otherwise tormented by the shapes of men and women, who were supposed to have power to haunt them invisibly, both in darkness and daylight. Often in the midst of their family and friends the children would pretend to be seized with strange convulsions, and would cry out that the witches were afflicting them.

These stories spread abroad, and caused great tumult and alarm. From the foundation of New England it had been the custom of the inhabitants in all matters of doubt and difficulty, to look to their ministers for counsel. So they did now ; but, unfortunately, the ministers and wise men were more deluded than the illiterate people. Cotton Mather, a very learned and eminent clergyman, believed that the whole country was full of witches and wizards who had given up hopes of heaven, and signed a covenant with the evil one.

Nobody could be certain that his nearest neighbour or most intimate friend was not guilty of this imaginary crime. The number of those who pretended to be affected by witchcraft grew daily more numerous ; and they bore testimony against many of the best and worthiest people. A minister, named George Burroughs, was among the accused. In the months of August and September, 1692, he and nineteen other innocent men and women were put to death. The place of execution was a high hill on the outskirts of Salem ; so that many of the sufferers, as they stood beneath the gallows, could discern their own habitations in the town.

The martyrdom of these guiltless persons seemed only to increase the madness. The afflicted now grew bolder in their accusations. Many people of rank and wealth were either thrown into prison or compelled to flee for their lives. Among these were two sons of old Simon Bradstreet, the last of the Puritan governors. Mr. Willard, a pious minister of Boston, was cried out upon as a wizard in open court. Mrs. Hale, the wife of the minister of Beverly, was likewise accused. Philip English, a rich merchant of Salem, found it necessary to take flight, leaving his property and business in confusion. But a short time afterwards the Salem people were glad to invite him back,

The boldest thing that the accusers did was to cry out against the governor's own beloved wife. Even the lady of Sir William Phipps was accused of being a witch, and of flying through the air to attend witch meetings.

Our forefathers, however, soon regained their senses, and became convinced that they had been led into a terrible delusion. All the prisoners on account of witchcraft were set free. But the innocent dead could not be restored to life ; and the hill where they were executed will always remind people of the saddest and most humiliating passage in our history.

The next remarkable event that took place while Sir William Phipps was Governor of Massachusetts was the arrival at Boston of an English fleet in 1693. It brought an army which was intended for the conquest of Canada. But a malignant disease, more fatal than the small-pox, broke out among the soldiers and sailors, and destroyed the greater part of them. The infection spread into the town of Boston and made much havoc there. This dreadful sickness caused the governor, and Sir Francis Wheeler, who was commander of the British forces, to give up all thoughts of attacking Canada.

Not very long after this, Sir William Phipps quarrelled with the captain of an English frigate, and also with the collector of Boston. Being a man of violent temper he gave each of them a sound beating with his cane.

But in this he was more bold than wise, for complaints were carried to the king, and Sir William Phipps was summoned to England to make the best answer he could. Accordingly he went to London, where, in 1695, he was seized with a malignant fever of which he died. Had he lived longer, he would probably have gone again in search of sunken treasure. He had heard of a Spainsh ship which was castaway in 1502, during the lifetime of Columbus. Bovadilla, Boldan, and many other Spaniards, were lost in her, together with the immense wealth of which they had robbed the South American kings.

Phipps was buried in one of the crowded cemeteries of London. As he left no children, his estate was inherited by his nephew, from whom is descended the present Marquis of Normanby. The noble Marquis is not aware, perhaps, that the prosperity of his family originated in the successful enterprise of a New England ship-carpenter, whose success began with his taking a prize from the sea.

LONDON: PRINTED BY
SPOTTISWOODE AND CO., NEW-STREET SQUARE
AND PARLIAMENT STREET

www.ingramcontent.com/pod-product-compliance
Lightning Source LLC
Chambersburg PA
CBHW031028120726

47905CB00007B/2083